CW00421949

BAPTISM OF FIRE

Reuben Cole - The Early Years Book 3

STUART G. YATES

Copyright (C) 2022 Stuart G. Yates

Layout design and Copyright (C) 2022 by Next Chapter

Published 2022 by Next Chapter

Edited by Tyler Colins

Cover art by CoverMint

This book is a work of fiction. Names, characters, places, and incidents are the product of the author's imagination or are used fictitiously. Any resemblance to actual events, locales, or persons, living or dead, is purely coincidental.

All rights reserved. No part of this book may be reproduced or transmitted in any form or by any means, electronic or mechanical, including photocopying, recording, or by any information storage and retrieval system, without the author's permission.

CONTENTS

1863 KENTUCKY

As the years rolled on, so did the War. Reuben Cole, still young, grew into a hardened, successful scout, trusted by those who rode alongside him, by the men who served in the ranks and by the officers who looked to him for help and guidance. Honing his skills, both in scouting and fighting, he donned buckskin clothes and exchanged his old Paterson for a brace of 1861 Navy Colts that several of his fellow troopers preferred. It was this gun that helped him overcome a desperado named Shapiro.

By now Cole was based in Camp Nelson in Kentucky, a sprawling collection of hundreds of buildings. Not only were there the usual barracks, mess houses, a makeshift hospital and jailhouse, but there were also additional constructions set up by private individuals. Saloons, eating houses, fruit and vegetable stalls, all thrived alongside the most popular of all businesses – the photography studio. Young recruits, eager to send mementoes back to their folks in faraway New York and Chicago, stood in long lines dressed in freshly pressed uniforms, some with their naturally blond hair dyed dark brown to show up in the final prints. Cole would watch them from afar, amused and always detached. He had no desire to have any memories of this ghastly war and his part in it.

Summoned to his Commanding Officer's quarters one morning, he stood with his hat clasped in front of him, studying the green-jacketed Sergeant-Major standing a little away from the Colonel's desk.

"This is First-Sergeant Cavendish of the Second Regiment of Sharpshooters," explained the Colonel without any preamble. "He and his men have been seconded to this post to aid us in the capture of a bunch of Rebel vagabonds who are raiding Union supply wagons and selling their wares to the Confederacy. So far, we have lost guns, ammunition of all types, and horses, of course. They need to be stopped."

Cole nodded. "And you want me to track 'em?"

"That's about it. Once they are located, Cavendish and his men will take charge. His orders are to destroy this gang with all due thoroughness. In other words, Cole – the Army wants them dead."

The Sergeant cleared his throat. "If I may, sir?" Colonel Mathieson nodded and sat back in his chair. "Except for their leader," said Cavendish, his voice unemotional. "A man called Shapiro. He is to be taken alive, if at all possible, and put on public trial so that the Rebs know we have broken up their operation."

"All right," said Cole. "Do we have any idea where these raiders might be?"

"Quite aways," said Mathieson.

"Mexican border was last we heard," said Cavendish.

Cole blinked and had to swallow hard before continuing. "*Mexican* ... but we can't go down there, Colonel! It's a journey of—"

"I know how far away it is, Cole," said Mathieson, leaning forward. "News came through from numerous sources so we're pretty sure it's accurate. Shapiro is holed up in a bordello not far from the Mexican border. It's in what we have come to know as the New Mexican Territory. You will travel with Sergeant Cavendish here and you will find him, extricate him, and bring him back. There is no other way to say this Cole – you have your orders, now get to it."

Cole had grown friendly with the small group of Indian scouts who were attached to the regiment. They were tough, small in stature but huge in courage. Most of them were Crow but one of them was Arapaho and his name, loosely translated, was Given Sky. It was always a name that intrigued Cole and when pressed, the young Indian finally relented and explained. "My mother would leave me in the center of our village when I was a tiny child, the world moving all around me without me noticing anything. All I would do, every day, was stare at the open sky. I felt so calm, the blueness so beautiful. I would never cry, not until she lifted me in her arms and took me into the wikiup. Then I would wail like a mad coyote. As soon as she took me outside to watch the sky, my cries would cease. She said, 'I will give you the sky' and that is what she did, through my name."

Cole loved that story. He loved those scouts, their easy manner, their calm resilience. When out on the trail, forever watchful, concentrating on every single blade of broken grass, every scuffed-up area of dirt; he'd learned so much from them. In the evenings they would sit, often not talking, and sink within themselves, pondering on the day they had spent and the next one to come. He liked that. It struck him that this kind of quiet reflection made them better scouts so he too took to following their example. The results, although not instant, certainly seemed to confirm his initial thoughts and as his skills developed, he honed to such a degree that even the Native scouts bowed to his greater insights and acknowledged him as the best among them.

It was a cold, grey morning a day or so before he was meant to leave when he came across Given Sky's body, stuffed behind some packing cases next to the Fat Belly Saloon. Wide-open eyes stared out from a stone-white face and the blood, which had spilt down from his ripped-out throat, dried black over his chest.

They said a wild dog, gone mad with disease, was responsible. But how could a dog then drag him behind those crates, thought Cole perplexed, as if hiding him from discovery?

"You found him easily enough, didn't you," asked Colonel Mathieson when Cole reported the Arapaho's death.

"It was dogs that led me to him."

"Well, there you are then," said Mathieson, leaning back in his chair, smiling like someone who had won first prize. "It's like I told you, them dogs, they can—"

"No," Cole snapped. Mathieson frowned. "No, the dogs did *not* kill him. I saw them sniffing around those crates, crates arranged in such a way to keep the body hidden from sight. Deliberately."

"You've been smoking with them savages too much, Cole. You know the stuff they put in them pipes makes you go loopy." To add emphasis, he put an index finger to his temple and made circular motions with it.

"So, you're not going to investigate it?"

"Investigate *what*, Cole? A drunken Indian set upon by a mad dog?" He leaned forward, gathering some papers as if suddenly they were his most pressing job. "Close the door on your way out."

"I'll take this to a US Marshal if I must."

Mathieson's eyes came up, narrow and dangerous. "I'll tell you what you will do, *Corporal,* you will keep your fat face shut. No one cares about some drunken savage, and I don't understand why *you* do."

"He was my friend."

Shocked at first, Mathieson's expression slowly changed to appalled. "I don't like you, Cole. I don't like the way you do things and I don't like the way you hang around that Redskin bunch the way you do. The only reason I don't pack your ass back to Kansas is that you are a damned good scout and we need you, more's the pity. Take my advice: go back to your bunkhouse and keep yourself low. I reckon if word gets out that you is preparing to bring in the law to sort this out, your life won't be worth a plug nickel."

"Is that right?"

"It sure as hell is! Now get out of my office!"

Outside again, Cole caught the eyes of three troopers glaring at him. He recognised them. A surly bunch who spent their days kicking the ground, playing cards and counting the days until they were discharged. He did not flinch from their glares. Instead, he stepped casually towards them, studying each one in turn. "If I find out it was you," he said, his voice low and steady, "I'll make sure justice is served."

"And how are you gonna do that, Cole?" asked the lean, dangerous-looking one in the center.

"I have my ways, Johnson."

"Oh yeah?" Johnson looked left and right to his surly companions. "My advice is to look out for yourself while out on the trail, Cole."

"Yeah," said one of the others, "all sorts of things can happen out there."

They all sniggered.

Cole waited until they were quiet again before adding, "Strange how you know what I'm talking about, isn't it Johnson?"

Johnson's face fell.

Cole turned about and, raging inside, strode back to his bunkhouse.

The following day the fort was full of the story about the troop of green-jacketed Sharpshooters who were going down south to

STUART G. YATES

sniff out Quantrill and his raiders. Cole did not enlighten them any further but wondered where the story had come from. As various ideas tumbled around inside his mind, he busied himself in preparing for the ride into Texas. As he checked through his saddle, Staff Sergeant Winter stepped up next to him. Winter was Cole's immediate superior, former Sergeant Burnside now fighting with the army in the east since his promotion. Cole immediately brought himself to attention.

"At ease, Cole." Winter reached out and smoothed his hand across the flank of Cole's horse. "I hear there was some nastiness the other night? You found a scout, murdered?"

"I believe he was, Sergeant, yes."

"You voiced your concerns to the Colonel, so I understand."

"Yes ... he, er, did not quite believe me."

"He's a busy man and has a lot on his mind."

"Yes, I expect he has." If Cole did not sound convinced, then that was precisely how he felt. He wanted to say more but kept his thoughts to himself for now.

"I'm not doubting you, Cole," continued Winter, "but if you can, put this to the back of your mind until your return. If foul play has occurred, I'll get to the bottom of it, have no worries about that."

Cole nodded. Winter spoke sense but Cole feared that if he managed to get through the hell that awaited him, the whole incident would have been conveniently forgotten. "If you wouldn't mind, sir, I'd like to make a report for the United States Marshal's office."

"We can handle this 'in-house' Cole, but if you are not satisfied with my own investigations, then you are free to do as you choose. I respect you immensely, young man, and your service is well-proven. So, let's see how it all pans out on your return."

Cole set his jaw, saluted, and watched the tall, lanky Sergeant stride across the parade ground. As he started to return to preparing his horse, he saw the three toughs who had already confronted him, leaning against a nearby hitching rail. Johnson

6

chewed thoughtfully on a strand of dry grass. His companions, thumbs in belts, glared. Johnson turned to a green-jacketed Sharpshooter close by and said something. They all laughed.

Ignoring them, Cole took his horse by the reins and led him gently away to where the hunting party was gathering.

ACROSS THE OPEN PLAINS

The journey, as they all knew it would be, proved long and arduous. Many times they had to make detours to ensure they were not spotted by Confederate troops. Texas, especially, proved the most dangerous, and it wasn't long before telltale signs appeared that they were being shadowed.

Cole held back his horse. He was ahead of the small column and slowed to allow Cavendish to come up beside him. Without looking at the Sergeant, Cole lowered his voice and said, "We're being followed."

Cavendish immediately stiffened and snapped his head around.

Calmly, Cole reached over and gripped the Sergeant's arm. "Don't make it so obvious. Relax."

"But who is it? How many?"

"I'm not sure but whoever they are, they are good. The fact that they haven't launched an attack makes me think they are a mix of Native people and renegades. There are not many Native peoples fighting for the Confederacy and even fewer here as we cross into Texas. They are almost certainly desperate, probably starving, and their interest will be on our supplies and horses."

"Will they attack?"

"Not a direct assault. An ambush." He nodded towards a far-off rock formation with towering cliffs and deep gullies. "There will be the perfect place."

"Then we'll simply go around."

"That will put hours if not days on our journey. No, best if I break off, circle wide, and come at them from the rear. I will need two men. Good men. Your best."

Cavendish did not look convinced as he chewed at his bottom lip. "Are you up to this Cole? I mean, you're nothing but a pipsqueak, how can you—"

"I believe I've proven my mettle, Sergeant, in matters such as this. More than once."

Cavendish caught the anger at the edge of Cole's voice. He blew out a loud sigh. "Very well. What should we do?"

"You make as if you are arguing with me, raise your voice, tell me to go to the rear as I am useless. Order two of your men – the men you have picked to be with me – to escort me as if under arrest. You can do that?"

"I can do whatever is necessary, Cole. Remember, *I'm* in charge."

"Yes, so shout, strike me if you must, then order those men to take me away. Do it now, Sergeant. Do not hesitate."

Perhaps relishing the task a little too much, Cavendish screamed out, "You damned rascal, Cole!" and struck him across the face. The blow was so strong it almost knocked Cole out of his saddle. "Fraser, Prentis? Come here, at the double."

Within a moment, two green-clad Sharpshooters reined in their horses next to Cole, who had a hand pressed against his bleeding nose.

"Take him to the rear and keep him there until I order you otherwise." He leaned forward and gripped Cole by the shirt front. As he did so, he whispered, "Prentis, this is a ruse, do you understand? When Cole gives the order, you follow them. Is that clear?"

"Yes sir," said the soldier called Prentis.

Cavendish pushed Cole away, "Get out of my sight," he yelled.

Prentis gave Cole a prod, took hold of his horse's reins, and led him to the rear. Every eye followed them with intense curiosity but neither of the two Sharpshooters reacted. At the end of the column, they stopped.

Cole sniffed loudly and stared at his hand, the blood smeared all over the skin. "He seemed to enjoy that."

"Cavendish is not a man to pick a fight with," said Prentis.

"Not unless you can handle it," put in Fraser, watching the other soldiers slowly moving forward. "What is this all about anyway?"

"We have company. Don't look; keep your eyes on me. We hold back a little, allow the others to get ahead, then we break away and make a wide detour."

Prentis grunted. "How many are we talking about?"

"I do not know. Could be half a dozen, could be twenty or more. We won't know until we come across them."

"This sounds like a plan doomed to failure."

"Well, it might be but we can't wait for them to attack. It will either be an ambush or a sneak attack at night. Either way, they will overwhelm us."

"All right." Prentis kicked his horse into an amble, Cole and Fraser moving in close behind.

Soon Cavendish and the rest edged farther ahead, out-distancing Cole and the others who continued to maintain unhurried progress.

The rocky outcrops were still a long way off when Cole signalled for the others to come to rest. "I'm going to make a break for it. Prentis, I'm going to knock you from your saddle. I'll then make a bolt for it. Frazer, aim your Sharps at my back but do not shoot." A tiny ghost of a smile played at the corners of his mouth. "Please."

Prentis, employing what he hoped was a believable piece of playacting, stretched out both arms. Cole pushed him in the side and Prentis fell, hitting the ground in a roll. Smacking his horse's rump with his hat, Cole galloped off while Frazer, good to form, drew out his Sharps from its scabbard and sighted along the barrel.

"Damn," he breathed, "it would be so easy to shoot him down."

Grabbing hold of the rifle, Prentis yanked it from the young soldier's grip. "We have to make this good but not *that* good!"

At an ancient dried-up river bed, Cole dismounted in the depression and got down amongst the rocks. His horse, well trained and possessed of unwavering trust, responded to Cole's tugging at the reins and obediently followed him to the ground.

Cole stroked the horse's neck. "Good girl, Candy. Good girl." Candy was his preferred mount and had been for some years now. It was moments such as this when he really appreciated the mare's intelligence.

He looked up as the others approached, slowing down as they reached the riverbed.

"Continue to move on," said Cole, waving them on. "Ride until I am out of your sight. Then wait. When you see me riding, fall in behind me. We'll then sweep around in a wide arc."

"I sure hope you know what you're doing," said Frazer.

"He knows," said Prentis, held Cole's stare for a moment, nodded, then moved on.

Cole watched them ride off. When they were nothing but smudges on the shimmering landscape, he rolled over and peered into the distance to where he suspected those following were based. He could see nothing, but an uneasy feeling playing around at the back of his neck convinced him they were there. Watching. Waiting.

He counted the seconds. With no timepiece, this was the only system he could rely on. "One-and-two-and-three," he said to himself, concentrating until he reached three hundred. Estimating this was around five minutes, he climbed to his feet, urged Candy to stand, and pulled himself up into the saddle.

Checking as he went, he rode in a northerly direction, well away from the others led by Cavendish. At one point, he dismounted amongst some sun-bleached boulders and scanned the landscape. He could see nothing to suggest he was being followed until, far away in the east, he saw the two Sharpshooters. He smiled to himself. The ruse could just work.

He stood up and froze.

Without turning, he knew someone was there. His stomach pitched over, his legs weakened. Slowly, he raised his hands and turned.

The Indian standing before him was dressed in rotten, filthy clothes consisting of threadbare buffalo pants and jacket, and a battered black felt hat crammed down over his head. Across his chest hung a pair of bandoliers, crisscrossed in Mexican style, cartridge cases catching the sun, in his hands a Spencer carbine. This was a man well-prepared for a gunfight. And now, he had Cole in his sights. Held loosely at the hip, the carbine pointed directly towards Cole's midsection. The one element of comfort was that the hammer had yet to be engaged.

"Drop your guns to the ground," he said, voice flat, unemotional. There was the faintest southern twang to his accent. He could have been from any one of the Five Civilized Tribes who fought for the Confederacy, but to find any this far south was a surprise.

Cole did as ordered, taking his time, anxious not to give any undue alarm.

As the gunbelt fell to the ground, the man edged forward and kicked it away. He surveyed Cole from head to foot. "You are not a soldier."

"I'm a scout," said Cole.

The man tilted his head. "Not such a good one. You did not know I was here."

"No. You're good. Very good."

"I trail your green soldiers, the ones you ride with. You are here to raid?"

"No, we are on our way to *find* a raider, a man who terrorizes women and children, burning farms, all of that. A dangerous man."

The man frowned deeply. "I know of no such man here." He brought up the carbine as his teeth flashed in an angry snarl. "You lie."

"No," said Cole, battling to maintain his control. A bead of sweat rolled down his forehead and dripped from his eyebrows. "His name is Shapiro. That is all I know about him except he is holed up close to the Mexican border and we are—"

The man gaped towards Cole, his eyes blinking rapidly. "I know him," he said and slowly lowered the Spencer. "He is a cruel killer who rapes and destroys without mercy. We fled from him. If you speak the truth..."

"I do," affirmed Cole.

"Then, I can help you. I know where he is."

A shot rang out, shattering the stillness of the moment. The bullet hit the ground next to the man's feet, throwing up a cloud of dust and broken stones. Reacting instantly, the man swung around, carbine coming up, eyes darting in every angle, searching the surrounding area.

"Drop that Spencer," came a voice, "or the next bullet hits you in the head."

Hesitating, the man snapped his head around to face Cole, who said quietly, "I'd do as he says if I were you. He doesn't miss."

Cole saw the fight leave the man's shoulders. He laid down the carbine and Cole moved close and picked it up.

A PARTNERSHIP FORGED

Approaching at a steady pace, Prentis emerged from his hiding place, a new cartridge already put into his Sharps rifle. Keeping his eyes firmly on the ragged warrior, he bent down and took up the Spencer. He threw it across to Cole, who gave a brief nod of appreciation. "Thanks."

"Don't mention it. Who is this?"

"They call me Ben Whitefoot," said the man dressed in the threadbare buffalo clothes.

"So," continued Prentis, unimpressed by what he had heard, "what do we do with him?"

"We see why he and his band are tracking us," replied Cole. He checked the carbine's load, grunted in satisfaction, and gestured for Whitefoot to move ahead.

It did not take long before they reached the camp. By the time they came upon the disparate collection of tepees, makeshift shelters and tree branches intertwined into paltry attempts at protection from the elements, Fraser had joined them. He kept his distance, wary of those around him. Mainly women, haggard, frightened children clinging to their mothers, and a few old men clinging onto life. They all sat amongst the debris of the camp. It seemed that Whitefoot was the only adult capable of putting up any sort of resistance. Even so, Fraser hung back, his rifle always at the ready.

As Cole walked through the camp, the women cowered away from him, the children's huge eyes staring out in terror from brown, gaunt faces as they watched him.

"What has happened here?"

Whitefoot tilted his head and frowned at Cole's question. "We are starving. There is no game here, the occasional buck-rabbit or prairie chicken if we are lucky, but not much else. The War does not go well and we have decided to move farther north, seek respite in one of the reservations. We saw you and thought you were a danger, raiders come to take what you wanted. But, as you can see," he waved his arm over the pathetic campsite, "we have nothing."

"We're not here to raid," said Fraser, his voice harsh.

Cole blew out his cheeks. "You say you know Shapiro, that you know where he is?"

"I have had dealings with him, as I told you. I know where he holes up when things do not go well for him."

"We don't need your damned help," spat Fraser, stepping forward to stand squarely in front of Whitefoot, glaring at him with barely controlled fury. He snapped his head towards Cole. "We don't need him, or his filthy family. Leave them here to starve is what I say."

"Fraser," said Prentis quietly, "pipe down a little. This man offers us no threat. If he can take us to where Shapiro is, that'll save us a lot of time and energy."

"No," said Fraser, shaking. "I'll not have a filthy savage in our ranks. And nor will Cavendish." He jutted his face towards Whitefoot. "You keep away from us, you hear me? If I spot you again, I'll kill you *and* your brood."

"You didn't spot him the first time," said Cole.

"Eh?" Fraser frowned at the scout. "What did you say?"

"You didn't spot him, I didn't spot him, and the only reason Prentis did was because Whitefoot here made himself known. If he hadn't, he could have picked us off one by one."

"That's bull, Cole. We knew he was here and we would have smoked him out. I mean, *look at him*! It would be as easy as pie to shoot him down."

"With that Spencer, he could have caused us quite a bit of trouble," said Prentis. "But he chose not to."

"What is this, Prentis? You an Injun lover, like this squirt here?" He jabbed his finger towards Cole. "You heard the rumor back in camp, that he's all busted up because of some mangy savage getting himself killed by some dog? Thinks it's murder. By golly, Prentis, if you wanna throw in with him, then you just do that but when the chips are down, I know who I'll be relying on – *me*! Not some scurrilous heathen, that's for sure. Leave 'em all here to starve is what I say, or maybe shoot 'em all dead."

"You've got a big mouth on you, soldier," said Cole softly. "My advice would be to keep it shut."

Fraser's mouth hung open. "What did you say to me, you damned child? What are you, eighteen? Has mama changed your diaper today? Because she sure as hell is going to have to if you keep talking that way to me."

"I told you to pipe down," said Prentis.

"You know what you can do, don't you Prentis?"

"Don't push it, Fraser."

"Or you'll do what?" He looked Prentis up and down, turned, and spat into the ground. "I'll bounce you and your friend all the way to the Mexican border if you rile me."

"Why don't you sit," said Whitefoot. "Talk with us. We can help."

"*Talk* with you? I wouldn't share a latrine with you."

Whitefoot went to speak but, without any warning, Fraser slapped him across the face with such force it almost toppled him. He staggered back, holding his face. Some of the women screamed, the children cried.

Cole moved. He took Fraser by the shoulder and pulled him around. "That's enough, you bastard."

Fraser's eyes flashed. He held his Sharps in his right hand and now, with his left, he swung a punch. Cole blocked it, wrapped his arm around Fraser's and jerked it tight. Fraser yelped, dropped the Sharps and tried to turn himself while bunching his right fist to aim another blow. Turning also, Cole snapped his left elbow under the man's jaw, released his arm, and landed a loping right into the side of Fraser's face.

Waltzing away drunkenly, Fraser went down, confused and bleeding. He sat there, staring at the ground as if he didn't know where he was.

Cole went to move in again, but Prentis held him back. "Enough, Cole. Enough."

Coming out of his blind rage, Cole stood blinking, struggling to recover his senses. He saw Whitefoot staring at him, confused. Perhaps no other white man had ever come to his aid before. Cole didn't know. He looked at Prentis. "Let's work out what we're going to do."

"I'll put you on a charge for that," shouted Fraser, getting uncertainly to his feet. "You're a Corporal ... what you just done, assaulting a lower rank, you're going to pay."

"Fraser," said Prentis, "you'll need witnesses for that and I didn't see a damned thing. Now, go and gather our horses and bring them back to camp. Do it *now*, soldier!"

They watched Fraser slink out of the camp, head down, hand pressed against his mouth.

"You can handle yourself, Cole. Where did you learn to fight like that?"

Cole shrugged. "A couple of years back, when I first enlisted."

"Well, remind me never to get into an argument with you." Prentis laughed and picked up Fraser's rifle. "The man's an idiot. He won't press any charges. He can shoot though, so ... watch your back when we come against Shapiro."

"You think he'll try something?"

"I wouldn't put it past him." He turned to Whitefoot. "Now, you tell us how we can find Shapiro and any other help you can give. In return, we'll give you and your people food and other supplies for your journey north."

Whitefoot did not speak; he merely stared before he crossed to the collected women and children, dropped to his knees, and embraced them.

TO THE BORDERLANDS

S tanding some way off, Cavendish regarded the soldiers loading up a pack animal with bedrolls, cooking utensils, and biscuits.

"We haven't any fresh meat," said Prentis to the small, ragged character whose eyes bulged with what was going on. "Maybe on the range, you can find game farther north."

"You sure he can help us?"

Cole cleared his throat. "Yes, Sergeant, I do. He seems to know a good deal about Shapiro, his methods, what he is capable of."

"And what did you say his name was?"

"Whitefoot."

"That's a strange kind of name. I've not had much dealings with savages, Cole. Everything I've heard about them is bad."

"I think that is probably true of most folk, Sergeant. All I can say is that in all *my* dealings with 'em, I've never come across any savagery. That is not to say it don't exist, mind. I have heard the stories so maybe there is some truth in 'em."

"If this all goes out of kilter, Cole, I'll hold you personally responsible. This is a hand-picked group of the finest Sharp-shooters from the finest regiment in the entire army. If anything should happen to them, it will be you who will face the consequences."

"I understand, but I see nothing in Whitefoot that causes me concern. The opposite is the case. He is desperate to do the right thing for his family. He will not jeopardize them by doing anything foolish."

"I hope you're right, Cole. At the first sign of treachery, I'll put a bullet in his brain. Understand?"

"I do, Sergeant Cavendish."

Later, having overseen his family's departure northwards, Whitefoot met with Cavendish and Cole to discuss plans.

"This is dangerous land," said Whitefoot. Cavendish sat in silence on a fragile-looking campstool, Cole standing at his shoulder. "Your men are easy to spot."

"What are you suggesting?" asked Cavendish.

"You tell them to take off their green coats. Ordinary clothes will not be so out of place."

"We're not raiders," said Cavendish, ruffled. "Nor are we spies. We are soldiers in the United States Army and therefore—"

"He makes a good point," interrupted Cole. "We can proceed in civilian clothing until we reach Shapiro's hideout. Then, your men can don their uniforms and present themselves as soldiers, not bushwhackers."

"We don't hide, Cole. This is a military operation."

"I understand that Sergeant, but we are operating in enemy territory. If we are spotted, then the whole endeavor could come tumbling down."

Cavendish folded his arms and stared at Whitefoot. "All right. But as soon as we are within spitting distance ..."

Whitefoot nodded, some of the tension leaving his face. "I think it will be the best thing to do. Cole and I will scout ahead."

"You know the way?"

Nodding, Whitefoot gave the faintest of smiles. "It will take us maybe three days, or nights. The heat and the chance of us being spotted, we should travel at night."

"I agree with that," said Cole. "With Whitefoot to guide us, we shouldn't have much problem traversing the route."

"I pray you know what you're doing in this, Cole."

"I believe I do, Sergeant." He turned his face skywards. "It will be evening soon. We should rest until the sun goes down, then start out again. Shall I tell the men?"

"I'll do it," said Cavendish, getting to his feet. "I have an uneasy feeling about all of this, Cole. Skulking around, pretending we are not who we are, is not something Sharpshooters do, Cole."

"And yet you hide amongst trees in woods," said Whitefoot. "Your fellow soldiers march over the fields and die in the face of guns."

"We are who we are," stated Cavendish, his voice trembling. "Sharpshooters. Our responsibility is to protect those fellow troops by seeing off Reb Sharpshooters, and cause as much disruption as we can in enemy ranks. We don't skulk, we fight and are highly trained to be the finest marksmen in the world. Best you remember that."

From that point, they travelled mostly at night, kept away from towns and encampments until, at long last, they crossed into the territory of New Mexico.

They followed the Santa Fe Trail and, not far from the Mexican border, they arrived in a decrepit old town, the towns-folk as bedraggled as the crumbling buildings in which they lived.

Finding shelter for their horses, Cavendish ordered guards to be set. "We're in hostile land, boys. Keep your wits about you."

Cole found a quiet corner and sat down in the corner of an old adobe building with no roof. Whitefoot decided he would rest outside, away from the others. Cole did not object. He had noted the animosity from the others. Apart from Prentis, who seemed a more enlightened and accepting individual, the Sharp-shooters displayed overt contempt, even disgust, that the Native trackers should have joined their troop.

The most verbal was Fraser, who now strode into the building in which Cole was trying to rest. "Do we have to have that savage trailing along beside us, Cole?"

Cole, the brim of his hat pulled down over his face, sighed but did not look up. "You mean Whitefoot?"

"I mean that filthy Indian, Cole." Fraser kicked at Cole's boots. "We're here now, so we don't need him no more. Send him away."

"We need him. As yet we don't know exactly where Shapiro is and until we do ..."

"We could ask the people here. They're bound to know."

Cole shrugged. "Give it your best shot, Fraser. You clearly don't like Whitefoot being part of our troop, so you do what you feel is best." To make it clear their conversation was over, Cole pressed his hat more tightly over his eyes and settled himself down to sleep.

"Damn you, Cole. Your arrogance sure as hell riles me."

Cole ignored him and it was only after the agitated Sharp-shooter left that Cole pushed up his hat brim and peered towards the open entrance. He knew for certain there was going to be trouble.

The sound of raised voices roused Cole from his sleep. Rubbing his eyes, he climbed to his feet and stepped out into the after-noon heat. Recoiling slightly, he leaned back against the wall of the building and screwed up his face. The heat was tremendous and Cole needed a drink. He shuffled across to the adjacent building, its paltry roof giving some shade and respite to the horses resting there. He found his canteen attached to the saddle at the horse's feet. He drank and stood, elbow propped against the animal's back, and sighed as his strength began to return to his weary limbs.

Again the shouting. He swung around and frowned into the distance. He made out a circle of men and, in their center, dust billowing around two others.

Cole gasped.

It was Fraser. He had Whitefoot by the throat and as Cole watched, the Sharpshooter slammed a fist into the Native's guts and followed up with a clubbing left to the head. Cole went to move but the large figure of Sergeant Cavendish emerged from the shadows and blocked his way.

"Leave it be, Cole. It's a soldier's fight."

Cole gaped at the Sergeant. "Are you insane? Whitefoot is no soldier. We need him, damn you!"

"No," said Cavendish, slowly easing out his Navy Colt from its holster. "Things have changed a little, Cole. We asked around and we've learned from some of the grizzled inhabitants of this stinking place, that a group of fairly despicable individuals are holed up in a place not so far away."

"Then why in the hell is Fraser beating down on Whitefoot?" Cole winced as Fraser hit the bedraggled Native again, dumping him to the ground. A hefty boot in the ribs hurled him away and he lay still, on his back.

"We caught him with a United States Remington Army revolver in his saddlebags. The Rebs ain't got firearms like that. He must have either stolen it from a Union soldier or picked it off of his dead body. Either way, he's a scavenger and as such he ain't got no place in this troop."

"But ..." Cole ran the back of his hand across his brow. "How did you find that gun, Sergeant?"

"Fraser found it and right now, as you can see, he's getting that filthy savage to tell us how he came by it."

Cole went to move but stopped when Cavendish brought up the Navy and cocked it fully.

"You'd be advised to sit yourself back down, Corporal, unless you want me to either shoot you for attempting to interfere or, as I just might do anyway, strip you of your rank. Perhaps, I might even do both."

Realising the futility of trying to stop what was happening, Cole stepped back into the shade and sank to the ground, back against the wall, close to the horses. He released a long sigh. "This is against all articles of war, Sergeant, as well you know."

"Indians ain't covered by articles of war, Cole. So, you just rest up and let us deal with the legalities. You get me?"

Nodding, Cole watched Cavendish disengage his gun's hammer and slip it back into the holster. "It shouldn't be long before we have the truth." Grinning, he turned around and marched across to where Fraser was delivering several more well-placed blows to Whitefoot's head. Cole closed his eyes and pondered on what he should do.

They strung Whitefoot up by the wrists and left him hanging from a tree branch, which creaked alarmingly as the stricken man's body swung with the wind.

Cole stood, peering up at him and felt the rage building up inside. There was laughter close by. It seemed that all of the soldiers involved in the beating were celebrating their actions. Cole bunched his fists.

"There is nothing you can do, Cole."

Cole turned his burning gaze towards Prentis, who stood before him, face awash with sweat. The day had moved on and the sun burned low in the sky but the air was thick with heat. "Wasn't there anything *you* could have done?"

"Like what?" asked Prentis, kicking absently as a stone. "Fraser found the revolver and Cavendish gave the order. I could not have prevented this."

"Fraser found the revolver ... do you believe that?"

"I don't know what to believe anymore. They beat the living

hell out of him and he confessed. Cavendish has ordered he be hanged. It's over, Cole. There is nothing anyone can do."

"Hanged? Hanged when?"

"Dawn."

"So they leave him like this until then?"

Prentis shrugged. "I'm not in agreement with any of this, Cole. The man came along of his own free will, in return for our assistance. But Fraser has it in his mind that this man is an infiltrator who will lead us into disaster."

"That's bull and you know it."

"It doesn't matter what I believe, Cole. I follow orders. That's it."

"That's a convenient excuse to hide behind, Prentis. You only follow orders? So what if it's an immoral order? What then?" He looked again at the battered Whitefoot. "You might, Prentis, but I sure as hell don't."

"What do you mean by that?"

Cole went to speak but stopped himself. He shot a glance towards Prentis and shook his head before he turned away.

DISCOVERIES AT DAWN

Something, not noise this time, awakened Cole with a start. He had not meant to fall into such deep sleep but exhaustion overcame him and he could not resist. Now, surrounded by a grey dawn, he sat up. Around him, Sharpshooters slept, many snoring. One of them should have been on guard duty, he realised and, suddenly afraid, he quickly pulled on his boots and stood up. Buckling up his gunbelt, he wandered outside, the cold biting into his flesh through the thin material of his shirt.

Squinting bleary-eyed, he crossed the hard impacted ground to where he hoped to find Whitefoot. His plan, which he had put together before he slept, entailed cutting Whitefoot down, putting him on the back of a horse, and setting him off across the prairie to meet up with his family travelling north. He had already gathered together some food and two canteens of water but now, angry at himself for missing the opportunity of following through with his plans under the cover of darkness, he broke into a run.

The tree stood black against the early morning sky, bands of purple and orange breaking up the iron-grey backdrop. At any other time, it could be classed as beautiful. The stillness of the air, the distant cry of a bird of prey hunting for its breakfast, the vastness of the rolling plains. All of it breathtaking. But of Whitefoot there was no sign.

Desperate now, Cole thrashed around, searching for the captive Indian. He had to be here. If he had managed to free himself, where would he go? The developing light aided Cole in reading the signs. He saw nothing that would lead him to suspect Whitewater had escaped. He saw the scuffed ground, the booted feet, the tracks of someone being dragged across the ground. Cole followed them and came to an outcrop of rock. He stood, mouth open, struggling to control his breathing. All of this reminded him of what he witnessed back at the fort. And when he moved closer and saw Whitefoot's body pushed in amongst the rocks, his body broken and bloody, his self-control deserted him and he dropped to his knees, looking at the murdered man's body, willing life to return, for his eyes to flicker open, for his voice to crackle and announce his relief at seeing Cole having come to rescue him.

None of those things happened of course. Instead, Cole stared at the corpse, those black eyes wide open, the mouth twisted in terror. Sometime in the night they had cut him down, dragged him to this place and dished out their own particular type of justice. A justice based, not on evidence, but on sheer prejudice and hate.

A footfall behind him.

Cole turned and went for his gun before realising he was far too late. Taken by surprise, his concentration on the battered body of Whitefoot, his senses frayed. He did not have a chance.

The riflebutt cracked into his face, and everything went black.

A deluge of water crashing over his face brought him awake again. Coughing and spluttering, Cole shook his head, rapidly blinking his eyes to try to bring everything into focus. He went to wipe his face with his hands but found he could not. His hands were bound tightly together. More ropes were lashed around his upper body, securing him against the same tree from which they had suspended Whitefoot. He twisted and tugged but the ropes proved too tight and as the face loomed over him, the fight went out of him and his shoulders slumped.

"Why in the name of God did you do it, Cole?"

Cavendish appeared genuinely shocked, his eyes wet with sadness, disbelief.

"I ..." Cole cleared his throat, struggling to find his breath. "I didn't, Sarge. I swear to God."

"You're a damned liar," spat Fraser, stepping g up next to Cavendish. Unlike the Sergeant, Fraser's face was contorted into a maniacal mask of fury and the spittle sprayed from his mouth as he spoke. "You sneaked out in the dead of night to do this, didn't you, you murdering scum!"

Cole gaped, too bewildered to offer up any form of defence. How could anyone believe that he was responsible? He strained against the ropes but to no avail.

"I saw you dragging him to those rocks," continued Fraser, the breath rattling in his chest, barely able to keep his temper under control. "I was too late to save the poor wretch. What did he have on you, Cole? Did he know what you had done back at the fort?"

"What?" Cole's voice splintered.

"We're going to have to investigate this, Cole," said Cavendish, taking a step away. "Unless you can give us an explanation for what occurred here, you will remain under guard until this business with Shapiro is done."

"But ... Cavendish, surely you don't believe this? Why would I ... it's insane!"

"For the reasons Fraser said perhaps," said Cavendish. He looked anguished. "I thought you were friendly with these damned Redskins? What possessed you to murder this one unless it's as Fraser says – he knew of your involvement in the murder back at the fort?"

"How could he?" snapped Cole, beginning to recover his wits. "He was not at the fort so he would have little idea of what went on there."

"How do we know?" spat Fraser. "Perhaps you're working for the Rebs. A spy, an infiltrator, undermining our efforts to inflict problems for the Reb army. Maybe that is why you were so eager to track down Shapiro. All of this was to lure us deep into enemy territory and then, what? Murder us?"

"You're insane, Fraser. Everything you say could just as easily be laid at your door, not mine."

"Yeah, but the problem is it was you who was caught standing over Whitefoot's dead body."

"Why were you here, Cole?" asked Cavendish. "I want to understand, I want to *believe* you had nothing to do with this."

"If I was a spy," said Cole, selecting every word with great care, "I would never have gone on missions into Reb camps and uncovered plots to attack our forces. I have worked tirelessly to unmask traitors in our mist, to bring them to justice, to save lives. The lives of our troops, Cavendish. Why would I betray everyone now? It just doesn't make sense."

"So, I'll ask you again – what were you doing out here in the middle of the night?"

Cole took in a deep breath. "All right. I'll admit I had a plan—"

"There you are," shouted Fraser, waggling his finger, "I told you! I told you he was planning on—"

"Shut up, Fraser," snapped Cavendish. "Let him speak."

"My plan," continued Cole, rattled by Fraser's outburst but managing to remain in control, "was to cut Whitefoot down, put him on a horse, and send him as far away as possible."

"Why do that?" hissed Fraser.

"Because he was already beaten, beaten almost to death. Now, why would anyone do that, eh, Fraser? Only someone with a burning hatred for Native Americans would undertake to beat that poor man to within an inch of death. He was no danger to anyone. You could see how he was suffering, hunger shrinking his limbs, his despair for his family eating away at him."

"He was a damned savage!" snarled Fraser, stepping up close to Cole. "And you, you damned Indian lover, you prance around as if you are the lord of all you survey. You talk to them as if they were human, as if all the murderous things they have done mean nothing. Well, let me tell you Mister God-Almighty, I've seen what they done. I've witnessed the burnings, the scalpings, the rapes. I've witnessed it first-hand and if I had my way, every last one of 'em would be strung up and left out for the buzzards."

"Or beaten to death like Whitefoot?"

"Yes! Why the hell not? It's nothing more than he deserved and if I had the chance to do it again, I'd ..."

His voice trailed away and he turned ashen-faced towards Cavendish who stood stoic and silent, eyes locked on the young Sharpshooter. "Is that what you did, Fraser?"

Fraser snapped his face from Cavendish to Fraser and back again and went to speak. No words came out of his mouth. He looked all around. His fist erupted into Cavendish's guts and the Sergeant yelped and fell. Drawing his revolver, Fraser turned it to Cole as voices rang out all around, *"Fraser! Drop that damned gun!"*

For one dreadful moment, Cole believed Fraser would shoot. Instead, the Sharpshooter broke into a mad dash towards the horses, vaulted onto the back of his own, and kicked it into a gallop.

Prentis ran up to Cavendish and helped him to his feet. "Sarge, are you all right?"

"I'll be fine. Only my pride is hurt. Cut Cole free and then take a couple of men and bring Fraser back here." He squeezed his eyes shut as he rubbed his stomach. "Alive."

TOWARDS THE BEAST'S LAIR

They waited until the early evening for the riders to return. Cole helped with burying Whitefoot. He was not familiar with burial rites for people from the Five Civilized Tribes or, in fact, *any* tribes. Now, standing over the finished grave, he hoped he had done the murdered warrior proud.

"There's still no sign of them," said Cavendish, words heavy in his throat. "I have a dreadful fear ... Cole, I apologise for the doubts I had about you. I should have listened to Prentis."

"Prentis?" Cole perked up at the mention of the young Sharpshooter's name. "Why? What did he say?"

"He spoke up about you, said you had ... what was the damned word?"

"Affinity," said Prentis stepping closer. "I said you had an affinity with Native peoples, that you saw them as a lot more than savages."

Cole smiled in his direction. "Thank you, Prentis."

"You can call me Sean." He held out his hand and Cole took it and shook it firmly.

"All of this leaves us in something of a pickle, Cole."

"How do you mean?"

"Well, with you and Prentis, I have only two other men. Five of us if the others don't come back. I'm not sure if that is enough to tackle Shapiro."

"It'll be enough," said Cole. "But who knows? Those others may well return soon."

"I'm not so sure," said Cavendish, looking out across the vastness of the empty landscape.

"Fraser is a desperate man," said Cole. "We need patience."

By the time nightfall descended, however, Cavendish had lost all sense of patience and paced around the ruins of the adobe building in which the remaining men were billeted. "We strike camp," he said at last from where he stood in the old entrance to the house. "We will travel through the night. I learned from some of the inhabitants of this forsaken place that Shapiro is holed up west of here in another crumbling pueblo. One of them has agreed to come with us, in return for a share of the reward put up for Shapiro's capture. We will have to approach with extreme caution. The villager says he has men with him. A gang of around a dozen."

He turned his grim face towards the others. A small, spluttering fire in the center of the hovel gave off an eerie light, casting Cavendish's face in deep shadow. His eyes and teeth glared out in a wild, disturbing way. "That means we are numerically at a disadvantage. Two-to-one. It is not great odds." He looked at them. "I'll go and talk to our guide, see if we can get going as soon as possible."

He blew out a loud breath and strode out into the developing darkness.

Next to Cole, Prentis stirred and got to his feet. He buttoned up his tunic. They had decided to confront Shapiro in their uniforms. Cole, wearing his buckskins, the one exception. He automatically checked the load of his Navy Colt.

Cavendish returned less than half an hour later, a small, wizened peon next to him. If anything, he appeared in a more desperate state than Whitefoot when they first came across him. A tiny man - his withered frame clad in a white shirt and trousers

- he wore a straw hat and threadbare sandals. A tasseled bag hung from his shoulders. He kept his eyes to the ground.

"This is Leon," said Cavendish. "He's half-Mexican. Not sure what the other half is but he seems honest enough and is keen to help his fellow villagers. He's the one who knows where Shapiro is. He said he is ready to go."

Prentis organised the few remaining men to prepare for their journey. Ammunition and that most essential of all supplies, water, were readied. Sharps rifles were checked, having been cleaned and oiled the night before. Cole did the same. His skill with the rifle was not as advanced as his companions and he knew his best contribution would be in close combat. He bore a pair of Navy Colts and had enough powder and shot to hold off a small army.

Walking amongst them, Cavendish appeared satisfied, nodding his head. He gestured towards Leon. "He rides on an old mule but don't let that fool you none. He knows his way through this country better than any of us. Always remember, boys, we journey through enemy land. If they catch sight of us, we'll have to fight to the last man. They won't show mercy, so neither should we."

He hauled himself into the saddle of his saddle and waited until the others mounted up. There was a light mood gathering amongst the men. They were exhausted but happy to be close to the end of their grueling journey.

The troop slowly made their way out of the decrepit pueblo, Leon at the front. Cole, like the others, did not speak. He turned his mind to thoughts of what might await them.

THE BEAST HIMSELF

They followed the little man in white who seemed to have endless energy. He did not falter or stop and continued at a steady pace; the only time he deviated to raise his canteen to his lips to take a small, occasional drink.

In a secluded dip, they made camp. By now they were deep inside what had long since been known as the New Mexican Territory and could relax, as almost all of the territory was under Union control. Meeting friendly comrades, however, was not automatic as the land was vast, the population small, and forts few and far between, most of them little more than hastily constructed palisades along the borders with Texas and Arizona.

Chomping through their meager rations, one of the men asked how Leon knew Shapiro. The man's demeanor changed, his expression haunted as he appeared to withdraw inside himself.

"Perhaps he doesn't want to talk about it," said Cole.

"No," said Leon suddenly, his eyes remaining focused on the ground, "it is not that ..."

Expectation of what was to come gripped them all.

Eventually, Leon spoke, his voice barely above a whisper. "It was not long before Glorietta Pass. My family and others had camped close to Pigeon's Ranch when the soldiers came. At least, we thought they were soldiers. We soon discovered this was not the truth. These men, they were not in any army that we knew of. Dressed outlandishly, with bright red shirts, blue neckerchiefs, huge floppy hats, they bore many pistols. They surrounded us. As we had no weapons, there was nothing we could do. They killed many of us, without any warning. They were wild men, laughing as they shot and knifed men and young boys. The women they took and raped many of them. My own wife ..."

For the first time he looked up, the tears spilling down his cheeks. "She died. I held her, weeping, as all around me these men, these beasts, they continued until, at long last, Blue soldiers came and drove them off." He undid his shirt and pulled it open to reveal two livid purple scars on either side of his navel. "They left me for dead. But God must have been with me that day as one of the Blue soldiers was a doctor. He took care of me together with the other survivors and saved my life. They asked me who was responsible and I recalled the voices of the men as they shouted, 'Hey, Shapiro, look at this one. She's plump, just the way you like.' That was my wife they talked about and Shapiro, he did not hesitate ..."

No one spoke. They continued to eat but half-heartedly now, and later they attempted to find sleep amongst the shade of miserable trees, bare of foliage. The heat increased with every passing moment and it proved impossible to rest. Cole, his thoughts on Leon, who sat apart, deep in thought. The man was no fighter, but he must have harbored a desire for revenge and Cole wondered how he would react once they captured Shapiro.

At long last, the night fell over them and, despite the Territory being less dangerous, they continued on their journey now that the air was so much cooler. They rarely spoke, the monotony of their route and lack of rest making them listless and irritable.

Several hours passed until the dawn lightened the sky.

Cavendish rode up to Leon and spoke to him. The little man barely reacted and after a short, almost one-sided conversation, Cavendish returned to Cole and Prentis.

"It's not far now, he says. If we play it right, we can surprise Shapiro at his breakfast." He smiled wryly. "At least that's what Leon tells me."

They came to a small cluster of houses, woodwork bleached white by the sun, nestling in a shallow dip in the landscape. Thin wisps of smoke came from a couple of dilapidated, flimsy buildings, tell tale signs that people lived there. Cavendish arranged his few men on the small rise overlooking what Leon had told him was Shapiro's hideout.

Checking his pistols, Cole watched the Sharpshooters preparing their weapons and, impressed by their professionalism, gestured towards the First Sergeant. "I'll come in from behind. When the shooting starts, they'll scatter, and I'll be close enough to get the drop on Shapiro." He reached inside his shirt and unfolded the wanted poster of the gang boss. "I've been studying this almost every night since we left Fort Nelson. I reckon I'd know him well enough."

"If any mistakes are made," said Cavendish, "I doubt anyone will hold us much to blame."

"I reckon," said Cole, putting the poster away again. Without another word, he turned his horse around and made his steady way to the far side of the tiny hamlet.

Securing his horse, he dismounted and moved across the broken scrub towards the rear of the three closest broken-down adobe buildings. A heavy silence settled over everything. Even the nearby horses, collected together inside a coral of misshapen pieces of timber, barely stirred as he approached.

Squatting down on his haunches, he drew one of his Navy Colts and shot a quick glance towards the ridge where Cavendish and his men waited.

Nobody had to wait long.

A man stumbled into view, stretching and yawning, a stone

jug dangling from his hand. He had no opportunity to drink from it as almost immediately a bullet smacked into his head and blew him backwards. The boom of the rifle round reverberated around the cluster of buildings and, within seconds, more men spilled into the open, whirling in all directions, disorientated, brandishing their revolvers wildly. Most were in a state of semi-undress, and they blustered about in total confusion, firing off their various pistols in any but the true direction of the Sharp-shooters.

More gunfire from the hillside dropped men with frightening regularity. And then he appeared, pulling on the braces of his canvas trousers. Shapiro. He ducked and dodged, running half bent towards the horses and even managing to struggle onto the bare back of one, firing off his gun, screaming for the remnants of his men to flee ... all of this before Cole stepped out from his cover and eased back the hammer of his Colt.

"Hold up, Shapiro," he shouted. "It's over."

Gawping as he battled to control his horse, Shapiro threw back his head and laughed. Eyes blazing, he brought up his gun in a blur. But Cole was faster and shot the outlaw through the right hand, shattering both trigger finger and thumb. He screamed, clutching at his shattered hand, blood spurting uncontrollably.

"Don't be stupid," said Cole, stepping up close to grip the reins, his Navy smoking, "or I'll kill you in your saddle."

Gripping his destroyed hand in a vain attempt to staunch the blood flow, the fight left Shapiro and he slid to the ground groaning. "You smashed up my gun hand real good, you miserable bastard."

Cole closed his eyes and blew out a loud breath before cracking his fist across Shapiro's jaw, sending him reeling backwards. "Don't tempt me to shoot apart the other one, boy."

Shapiro blinked back tears. "I'll learn to shoot with my other hand and I'll kill you dead."

Cole smiled. "If you live that long."

Shapiro went to respond but the effort proved too much and, instead, his eyes rolled into the back of his head as he keeled over sideways and slipped into unconsciousness.

RETURN TO NELSON

They all knew the return journey would be dangerous. Passing through Texas, even if only for a few dozen miles, meant running a deadly gauntlet. As before, they decided to travel at night but at their first camp, trouble was already brewing.

Shapiro, bound and gagged, his wounds tended to, sat with his back to a nearby tree. Despite the shade, the sweat poured down his face, most of it evaporating before it dripped onto his vest. Cole knew this to be dangerous. Loss of moisture could prove lethal if not controlled by plenty of water. Although each soldier had two canteens, finding sufficient water to replenish supplies was not easy. Most streams were dry and the few tributaries they came across were saline.

"I have spare water," said Leon on the second morning. He had observed Cole going to the captured Shapiro and tipping his canteen to the man's mouth to give him small amounts of liquid, enough to keep him alive.

"Where did you get that?" asked Cole.

The little man shrugged. "I've lived around these parts all my life. I know how to conserve water."

Sighing, Cole nodded. Perhaps his faculties were not what

they should be given the intense heat. He simply wasn't thinking straight in allowing Leon to go to their prisoner.

He heard the scream, snapped his head around and watched in horror Leon drawing a long, gleaming blade. He dashed across the short distance separating him from where Shapiro was lashed to the tree. He caught Leon by the wrist as the little man was poised to strike, Shapiro cowering in terror as his life must have flashed before him.

Twisting his arm, Cole turned Leon around and flattened him with a tremendous punch in the jaw. The little man collapsed and just as others arrived, Cole took the heavy-bladed knife from the man's hands and tossed it away.

Breathing hard, Cavendish appeared, assessing the situation quickly. He checked Shapiro and, satisfied that the renegade had sustained no injuries, fell onto the ground. "Well done, Cole! I do not want this man to be a victim of another's vengeance, no matter how justifiable that may be. I want to see him dangling from a rope, his crimes documented and his guilt reached by law." He reached forward and clamped his hand on Cole's shoulder. He smiled. "We'll keep Leon under close guard and return him to his family. We shall continue to Nelson and bring to an end this terrible episode."

A deep sense of depression descended upon the men from this point. Before the attack on Shapiro's camp, there was a strong sense of duty reverberating amongst them. Now, with the renegade safely secured on the back of a bedraggled mule, anticlimax clawed away at their very souls.

It was in this low state that they came across a miserable group of Mexicans scratching out a living amongst the cruel, hard conditions. Cole, riding ahead of the troop, spotted them first and went to them, his hand raised in peaceful salutation. The men, toiling in their fields, stopped and leaned on their farming tools, watching Cole's advance with worried expressions. Making sure his hands were well away from his Navy Colts, Cole reined in his horse and dismounted. He approached the group slowly, arms spread out.

"Don't be alarmed," he said and smiled.

Beyond the men, several women, some clutching children to their bosoms, appeared through the entrance of a squat, badly built dwelling. Apart from the open doorway, there was only one small window hacked out in the facing wall. The roof, if it could be called such a thing, was made from interweaving bleached tree branches with bracken stuffed in the gaps. Cole doubted it would stand for more than a handful of weeks. If rain came, it would be washed away. He had heard of pueblo Indians from this region living in adobe buildings that they would simply rebuild if the rains came. Perhaps these people were the same.

It was then that he spotted one of the women holding an ancient, muzzle-loading carbine. She eased back the hammer, which made an ominous and loud click. Cole raised his hands. "Hey, I'm not here to cause trouble!"

None of the people facing him seemed to be convinced by his words. One of the men passed his spade to a companion and came forward. He stood not six paces from Cole and blabbered away at him in what Cole assumed was Spanish. All he knew of that language was the ubiquitous *por favor*, which he now repeated several times.

Behind him, the rest of the troop slowly arrived. Cole turned to them and signalled for Leon to come forward. "The rest of you stay where you are."

Reluctantly at first, Leon approached. After he dismounted, he came forward and engaged the others in their language. After what seemed to Cole to be a heated exchange, Leon turned and glared. "These people are deeply afraid of strangers. They traveled from Mexico to settle here and since arriving have had many dealings with Navajo who come and steel their sheep, ruin their crops. So they have moved on, hoping to find somewhere safe. But the threat of raiding parties is always with them. They want to know what you want."

"Nothing," said Cole. "Maybe a place to rest up until night falls. We must be close to the border by now."

Another conversation between Leon and the Mexicans took place. Cole strained his ears in an attempt to gauge some meaning from the words. He failed and, sighing, he again had to wait until Leon spoke to him.

"They have met Union soldiers who have promised them protection. There are moves to launch an attack on the Navajo, they have been told, and force them to relocate north to a Federal reservation. He does not believe that has happened yet. Some of his family do not believe it will ever happen."

"For tonight, at least, we can offer our protection."

Leon's eyes narrowed as if Cole's words were false. Shaking his head, he conveyed those words and, perhaps, his reservations. The man listened and eventually nodded. Cole and the Sharpshooters could make camp close by but it would be preferable if they left as soon as possible afterwards.

Cavendish, who had already made the decision to move on early before the sun loomed too high, ordered the men to bed down. Horses needed to be fed and watered first and as Cole and Prentis did so, the young Sharpshooter pulled Cole to one side. "I'm not sure if I trust Leon any longer. He's changed since Shapiro has come into our camp. We'll need to watch him."

"You're right. I'm not entirely sure that he translated exactly the conversation he had with the head of this Mexican group. Seems that trouble has occurred between themselves and the Natives for quite some time."

"Yeah, well, it *is* their land."

"Exactly." Using a clump of straw, Cole wiped down the flank of his horse then put a feed bag around its nose. Without a pause, the animal began to munch through the grain inside. "I've had dealings with Kiowa but not Navajo. I'm guessing they are similar but the war has shook everyone up and these people, I feel, have been badly affected. Scraping a living the way they do, you have to admire them."

"It's a wonder to me the Navajo have not murdered them all by now."

"They're raiders, so maybe without these people they too would starve. It's a complicated life out here, as well as a dangerous one."

"For me, I would rather be back in Kansas. I'm not sure how my particular skills with a rifle will help me out in finding suitable employment but something will crop up, I am sure of it. What about you?"

Cole paused. He leaned against his horse, draping his arms over the animal's back, listening to it eating. "I'm not rightly sure. Like you, I doubt my skills will be in demand when this damned war is done. Maybe I'll stay on in the army, be a scout. I'm fairly certain that our Indian troubles will not cease merely because we Americans have decided to stop killing one another."

"You think it ever will end? The Rebs have a flair for hanging on."

"They are fierce fighters, that's for sure. What is required, I guess, is a decisive battle, defeating them on such a scale that they lose the capability to recover."

Both slipped into quiet contemplation as they continued to care for the horses, moving to the others one by one until all were wiped down. Retiring to the camp, they settled down. Cavendish sat a little way off, propped up with his saddle, smoking a pipe.

"You boys did well, I've put Lomax on guard duty. I'll relieve him in a couple of hours, then perhaps one of you could take over from me?"

"I'll do that," said Cole quickly. He smiled across at Prentis. "We're pretty much bushed, Sergeant, but we'll do our best."

"That's good enough for me, Cole." He tipped his head back and stared at the darkening sky. "This is a beautiful country, boys. One well worth fighting for. My only prayer is that we all live to enjoy it."

"A-men to that," said Prentis as he settled himself down.

Cole studied his new friend, then turned to Cavendish. "When we pull out tomorrow," he said quietly, "what do you think will happen to the Mexicans?"

"Who knows? Living out here with no protection, I don't give all that much for their chances. I've heard about them Navajos. Mean."

"Everyone is *mean*, Sergeant, when they are defending what is their own. They been fighting in this land for centuries. I don't see it ending soon. It'll be like the war, going on and on and on."

Cavendish grunted, knocked out his pipe and, pulling his hat over his face, snuggled down under his blanket and went straight to sleep.

ATTACK

U nlike before, there was no particular sound that brought Cole awake but more of a feeling of dread. Through the night, dreams troubled him. Strange, distorted images of his father and mother, especially of his mother with her hands reaching out, imploring him to "stay safe my precious boy". Such images disturbed him greatly. He could not remember the last time he had dreamt of her nor, indeed, anything to do with home. Drenched in sweat, he sat up, gazing into the enveloping darkness, his heartbeat pounding in his head. Around him, nothing stirred, the silence deep and threatening. He sat alert. Inching his fingers to the Colt Navy he kept under his rolled blanket pillow, he got to his feet and stood, waiting.

Over against the black outline of a tree, he thought he could pick out Cavendish. Squinting through the darkness, he wasn't sure. Beside him, within an arm's reach, Prentis slept, his breathing heavy and even. He considered waking him but then a noise came from far off. Not distinct or obvious, more a muffled grunt. Perhaps it was a buffalo snooping through the camp. Cole was not about to take any risks. He eased back the hammer of his gun and crept over to where he believed Cavendish to be.

Sure enough, he found the Sergeant asleep, a rumbling growl

coming from his chest. Nothing short of an earthquake was going to wake him thought Cole as he slowly scanned the surroundings. The grunt troubled him and he listened out for another but it did not come. Had he imagined it, his mind already in disarray after his dream? He went to drop his Colt into its holster when he heard it. Not a grunt this time, a definite cry. A cry of pain.

Instantly, Cole went down on one knee, Colt ready. Allowing his mouth to hang open so he could focus his hearing, he again waited. Nothing else came out of the darkness; nevertheless, he moved forward, cautious now, taking his time, each step soft. He headed for where he believed Lomax to be.

His eyes grew accustomed to the gloom. He made out trees and the outlines of rocks. Lomax would have made for the slight high ground not far from where the Mexicans lived. From there, the view afforded by such a vantage point was all-encompassing. Even in the dark, it would be easy to spot any movement from strangers or would-be raiders.

Unless they were well versed in deception. The Navajo were excellent fighters, their skill in ambush well known throughout the Indian Territories. If they had encircled the camp without being seen, which was entirely possible, the ensuing fight would be difficult.

Something moved ahead. Flattening himself to the ground, Cole cursed himself for not summoning Cavendish and Prentis to help. On first awakening, he was not convinced the sounds were made by Navajos. Now, he wasn't so sure.

The still air crackled and fizzed with expectant energy, almost as if the atmosphere were charged as it often was before a storm.

Squinting, he thought he could see a shape, nothing more than a smudge against the sky. It was impossible to see if it was the outline of a person, an animal, or perhaps a bush. He was not about to take any risks. Holstering his gun, Cole brought out his knife. Ten inches of honed, heavy steal. He slithered forward snake-like. His approach was slow, ponderous even, but he had little choice. If Navajo warriors were close by, as soon as he stood, they would spot him and attempt to kill him. So he edged ever closer on his belly, the sweat beading down his face, his heartbeat loud in his ears.

The shape was not a man. It was three men and one of them was Lomax. Two warriors had him pinned down and were taking his scalp. Cole prayed he was already dead. The young Sharpshooter made no sound, an impossibility if he remained alive through the horror of having his hair cut from his head. Cole thanked God for that.

Ten paces away, Cole checked all around him. There would be others, of course, skulking in the darkness. He doubted two men would make a raiding party. One of the warriors stood to his full height and stretched his arms skywards, brandishing the dripping scalp in one hand and Lomax's Sharps rifle in the other. A signal for his companions no doubt.

Cole counted to ten. No one emerged from the depths of the night so, continuing to concentrate on what had happened to Lomax, he moved forward, a ghost, soundless.

Turning the knife, he slammed the tip of the handle underneath the closest warrior's ear, felling him like his legs had been chopped off at the knee. In a fluid, flowing movement, he sank the blade deep into the second warrior's guts and sliced it across to the left, opening him like a bloated fish. Blood and entrails slipped out over Cole's fist.

He did not pause. Turning, he dispatched the first warrior with a powerful thrust into his throat. Both men died at Cole's feet as he stooped to check Lomax. The poor man still lived, eyes white and wide in his horrorstricken, blood-spattered face. Cole knew there was nothing he could do. The man was in shock, so he was not aware of what they had done to him. He would die soon. Cole cupped his hand behind the man's head, trying his best to give some comfort. Then the light went out of his eyes and Lomax died.

Cole continued to hold him. None of this was meant to happen. The Navajo must have been desperate beyond imagining to revert to this level of savagery. And Cole himself had plunged into the depths of murderous rage, revisiting the basest level of his inhumanity. Bowing his head, he pressed his finger and thumb into his eyes and wept.

He was not yet twenty years of age.

Orange light caught his attention as he got to his feet, trembling with the violence. It glowed across the sky and could mean only one thing. The Navajos had attacked the Mexican encampment. Returning the knife to its sheath, he drew both Navy Colts and moved forward.

With each successive step, the sounds of the attack increased. The screams of women and children, the roars of men, the occasional blast of a gun. And everywhere, wild gyrating shadows, shapes of men, hungry, incensed warriors raising hatchets and knives, blades flashing in the fetid air thick with smoke and flame.

He fired his pistols. There was no need to remain in the shadows any longer. So, he shot the attacking warriors without hesitation, easing off gunshots with calm, calculated accuracy, wounding or killing them with detached ease. By the time he came to his last round, five semi-naked warriors were lying stretched out on the ground, bodies perforated with bullet holes. None of them would be getting up again. Those who managed to survive ran into the night, screaming in terror. They would forever remember the nightmare of this fight.

As would Cole. With the shadows of people milling around him, he fell to his knees and stared into nothingness, appalled at the excesses of what he had done.

DAWN'S PEACE AND MORE

As the dawn illuminated the extent of the attack, everyone pitched in. Smoke continued to belch from the remains of the homestead, flames licking around the blackened timbers. Navajo bodies were put into a pile and set aflame. Two women, an elderly man, and a tiny child of no more than two years were buried and words said over their graves.

"You shouldn't be so hard on yourself, Cole," said Cavendish, his shirt sleeves rolled up past his impressive biceps. "You did what you had to, nothing more."

"I killed more of them than they did us," said Cole, subdued. "Nothing is going to change that."

"Reuben." It was Prentis, also stripped of his green jacket, his grey shirt turned black with sweat. "If you had not done so, none of these people would be alive. The children would have been taken, the women ..." Shaking his head, Prentis turned away.

"He's right, Cole," said Cavendish. "We have all suffered since leaving Nelson. We are the only three who remain out of our original troop and God alone knows if we will make it back." Dragging his forearm across his brow, he walked away, eyes downcast, silent.

· · ·

Sometime later they stood in quiet contemplation, the one sound so awful it set Cole's teeth on edge. Family members wailed in total grief at the loss of their loved ones. As the acrid smell of the dead Navajo's funeral pyre filled the air, the scene could have come straight from the pages of Saint John's Revelations. Cole had little doubt that the Apocalypse would be much like this.

"Let's get out of here," said Cavendish, replacing his kepi.

Cole and Prentis fell in line with Leon some way behind. No one dared look the remaining Mexicans in the eye.

"We were meant to help them," said Cole as he climbed into the saddle. "Instead, we have allowed their lives to be destroyed."

"They would all have died if it had not been for you, Cole," declared Prentis, kicking his horse into a steady walk.

Behind the Sharpshooter, Shapiro, well bound with leather cords, rode on his horse tied to Prentis's saddle.

"Perhaps it would be best if they had all died," said Cole.

"Death is never good, Cole," said Cavendish, who was at the head of the small column. He twisted in his saddle to reveal a face drawn and haggard. "God knows I've had to suffer its consequences too many times." His eyes flashed ferociously as he glared at Shapiro. "Damn this war, and damn all those who revel in it."

Throughout the journey, Leon remained in a subdued mood and did not utter a single word. His family had already been relocated to one of the smaller reservations in the north and, upon their arrival at Fort Nelson, the first thing he did was seek out which one it might be.

He left almost immediately, granting Cole the merest of nods in what was hoped to be some sort of gratitude. Cole returned it with a half-smile before he went to the livery to ensure his horse was well catered for.

Prentis joined him there. "I've just put Shapiro into a holding cell. He's a surly es-oh-bee that's for sure. No remorse, not a flicker of regret."

"Let's hope justice can be served for all the things he has done."

Nodding, Prentis turned his eyes away. He appeared pensive.

"What's wrong?" asked Cole.

"We must attend a so-called debriefing with Colonel Mathieson."

Cole put his forehead against his horse's flank and groaned. "Do we have to?"

"I'm afraid so. He wants a detailed report of all that happened down in New Mexico before he interrogates Shapiro."

"I need to go and speak with Sergeant Winter first. The Colonel will know all about it. I want to know what's been done about Given Sky's murder."

"Who's that?"

"A friend. I found him ... ah, never mind that. I'll talk to Winter first and see if he is any closer to discovering who the perpetrators are."

"Winter isn't here, Cole."

The scout lifted his head. "What do you mean, he isn't here?"

"Well, to be absolutely accurate, that's not exactly true. He is here, but ..."

"Sean, you ain't making much sense."

"I'm sorry ... Winter is dead, Cole. His body is at the surgeon's, awaiting burial."

"Awaiting burial? What happened?"

"Not long after we set out, he was found hanging from the rafters of his bunkhouse." The Sharpshooter shook his head. "He killed himself, Cole. Suicide."

Seated at the head of the long highly polished table in a room adjacent to his office, Colonel Mathieson read through the report submitted to him by Cavendish. Occasionally, he would make tiny guttural noises from the back of his throat but for the most part, he showed no emotion until he came to the end. He then slowly reshuffled the papers, knocked them square, and placed them face down on the desk. Leaning back, he regarded each of the three men in turn.

"How would you say Shapiro is ... as a human being?"

Cavendish, a little taken aback by this question, blinked rapidly and looked to the others for support before he shrugged and said, "He's a killer, sir. He has no conscience, no honor."

Mathieson nodded. "He made no show of admitting any of the things he has done?"

"None whatsoever."

"Problem is, Sergeant, most of the evidence against this man is circumstantial. Hearsay. I trained as a lawyer back in New York City before the War. I know something of these things. Unless we have witnesses, there is very little we can try him for. He will be classed as a prisoner-of-war and when the deprivations of this dreadful conflict are at an end, he will be released." He folded his arms. "For me, that is not a satisfactory conclusion. Would you agree?"

"We have Leon," said Prentis quickly. "He has first-hand experience of what Shapiro did."

"That half-breed?" Mathieson shook his head. "He's gone. Left to meet up with his family."

"Could we not fetch him back for the trial?" asked Cavendish.

"From what I can see, and from reading this," he waved Cavendish's report, "we don't have enough to send Shapiro to the gallows, with or without that half-breed's evidence, not that I think the court will take his evidence into much consideration."

"Why not?" asked Cole.

Mathieson's eyes narrowed. "You, as an Indian lover should know one thing, Cole. You are in the minority."

"That doesn't make me wrong."

"It makes you an insubordinate, arrogant bastard."

"Sir!" said Cavendish. "I must protest. Corporal Cole has exhibited great courage throughout the expedition. He single-handedly thwarted an Indian attack on the Mexican settlement we came across."

"*Mexican* settlement?" Mathieson shook his head. "You're as bad as him, Cavendish. My advice to you is to take your man here and return to your encampment in Kentucky. You've done your best; now it's time for you to leave."

"I've lost a lot of good men, sir. I want to know that their deaths were not in vain. I want to see Shapiro put on trial, found guilty, and publicly hanged."

"That is not going to happen, Cavendish. He'll serve some time but not a great deal. Justice, gentlemen, will *not* be served."

A deep gloom descended over the assembled men until Cavendish signaled to Prentis that they should leave. Cole remained behind, waiting until the others had gone. Then he slowly turned to Mathieson, who continued glaring at him.

"I take what Cavendish said about you, Cole. You have more than proven yourself a brave and dependable soldier. You do know he has commended you for a promotion? Put it in writing and presented it to Washington? No doubt you will receive their decision in due course. Until then, you go about your duties and await further orders. Dismissed." He returned to the report and, without reading it again, slipped it into his tunic.

"What happened to Winter?"

As if struck across the face, Mathieson flinched and gaped at the young scout. "Winter? What about him?"

"Rumour has it that he hanged himself."

"It's no rumour, Cole. He was found in his quarters, hanging from the—"

"I know where he was found and the circumstances surrounding his death. *Supposed* circumstances."

"What the hell is that supposed to mean?"

"I don't believe it."

"Oh, and who are you to say what is what? God Almighty?"

"No, sir. I'm just concerned is all. Concerned that there are elements within this fort that, how shall say it, are undermining the very fabric of your command."

Mathieson leaned forward. "Are you out of your mind? First of all, you didn't accept the reasons for your Indian friend's death and now this. When Washington contacts me about the possibility of you being promoted, I shall tell them with no hesitation that you are unfit. You are unpredictable, lack discipline, and hold great contempt for your superiors. A good scout you may well be Cole, but as a member of any troop, you cannot be recommended. You're a loner, do things your own way and, as such, are a threat to the wellbeing of my men. You let Fraser get away and that led to the loss of two Sharpshooters. That is on you, Cole. I'll make damned sure nobody forgets that."

Cole listened to this tirade in stoic silence. As Mathieson came to the end of his speech, Cole drew in a deep breath. "I understand his wife is coming across from Louisville and will arrive in the next day or so."

"And?"

"I shall talk to her, Colonel. Find out exactly what sort of man her husband was."

"My advice would be to keep your nose out of this, Cole. You may discover things that you'll live to regret."

"Is that a threat?"

Mathieson sprang up, red-faced, brandishing his fist. "You're an insolent cur, Cole. I'll break you if you continue along this course."

"I don't believe Winter committed suicide," said Cole, unabashed. "Nor do I believe Given Sky was mauled to death by dogs. Both men were murdered, Colonel, and I mean to find out who is responsible." It was his turn to lean across the desk. "You try and stop me, Colonel and you'll find out just how unpredictable I can be."

"I'll have you arrested and flogged for this!"

"On what charge? Honesty?"

"Insubordination."

Standing up, Cole looked around him and made a grand, theatrical sweep with his hand. "Witnesses, Colonel? Even in the army, it'll be my word against yours. No, the point is, if you won't do anything to get to the bottom of Winter's death, then it'll be up to me. And I won't stop until I find the culprits, no matter what it takes."

Outside on the porch, Cole leaned against a post propping up the veranda shade and let out a long sigh. He watched as soldiers and civilians alike went about their daily business, all of them oblivious to what had occurred. Would any of them care if they knew, he pondered? There was only one person who did care, and that was himself. He was going to find out the circumstances of Winter's death and that of Given Sky. He felt sure they were linked. His one problem was to prove it.

INVESTIGATIONS BEGIN

On the morning of his departure, Sean Prentis found Cole at the livery stable where the young scout was repairing a saddle.

"We'll be leaving directly, Cole," said Prentis.

Cole stood up and took the Sharpshooter's hand. "It was an honor to ride with you, Sean."

"That is mutual. You watch yourself, Cole. There are a lot of people around here who would prefer you to live your life in the shadows."

"I know. Problem is, if there is an injustice, then I must face it down."

"I wish I could stay behind and back you up, but we have orders. Cavendish and I are going out west. The war is not going well for the Rebs, but they are not beaten yet, so we have much to do."

With that, after a final shake of hands, Prentis moved away, leaving Cole wondering if he would ever meet the young Sharp-shooter again.

. . .

He gave Sergeant Winter's wife time to move into the quarters set aside for her before he politely rapped on her door. Her companion, a much younger woman, stared wide-eyed at Cole as he stood in the entrance. He quickly pulled off his hat and, clutching it in both hands, bowed slightly. "Sorry for the intrusion, ma'am."

"It's *Miss*. Miss Dryson."

Her blue eyes twinkled with youthful enthusiasm, coupled with assertiveness and strength. Cole felt his cheeks grow hot and he could not hold her stare. Clearing his throat, he shuffled his feet and tried to gather himself. This proved more difficult than he could imagine. She was quite lovely and her smile as it spread across her mouth, open and welcoming, caused his heart to pound.

"Can I help you with anything?"

He wasn't sure anymore. Wilting under her relentless gaze, he heard himself muttering incomprehensible garbage. She laughed and he stepped backwards, cramming his hat back onto his head. "I will ... I ..."

Her laughter rang in his ears as he whirled around and ran off, feeling as if he were fourteen again.

He lay on his bunk, staring at the ceiling, his mind alive with images of her. Miss Dryson. The feelings coursing through his veins were unlike anything he had ever experienced before. Girls, *women,* they were another species. Unknown, unfathomable. He remembered sitting with his mother one evening. She was so ill then but had somehow managed to muster the strength to come down and sit with him beside the fire. The logs crackled and popped as she bent her head over an embroidery, working at it in silence, her concentration etched into every furrow of her brow.

"Ma," he said quietly.

She looked up instantly. She always had time for him, no matter what she was doing or whatever the time of day. She smiled expectantly.

"Can I ask you something?"

"You can ask me anything you wish, Reuben."

He shifted uncomfortably in his chair. "I ... I don't really know where to begin. You'll think me an idiot."

"That is something I will never say or think about you, Reuben."

Another smile. Cole allowed himself to relax a little. "I went into town with the Rushton brothers the other day, to get supplies, wire and nails and stuff and ..." He blew out a breath and wiped his mouth with his hand. "We were in Simpson's Merchandise Store and while the brothers were buying the things we need, these two ladies came in and—"

"Ladies? How do you know they were ladies, Reuben?"

"They was dressed real neat, Ma. In full, flowing dresses with frilly sleeves and bonnets as wide as a room."

She laughed. "You should be a poet, Reuben. You're good with words."

"Ma, I'm being serious."

"All right." She put her embroidery down. "Tell me what's on your mind."

"It's just that, well, what I mean is, they was mother and daughter. I could see that. They were both dressed the same but the older one, well, she was just *a mother.* But the younger one ... ah, Ma, she was *so* pretty. I ain't ever seen anyone so pretty. And she caught me staring and she smiled at me! I mean, she smiled, Ma! At *me.*"

"And why do you find that so extraordinary, Reuben? You're a handsome young man."

"Ah, Ma! Stop."

"It's true. Look at you, growing to be so tall and straight. You're strong, have a fine, handsome face with that firm jaw. You're just like your father used to be when I first met him. I didn't believe I had ever seen anyone so fine, dressed as he was in his best Sunday clothes." For a moment her eyes seemed to drift away as the years disappeared and she was a young girl again. "I fell in love almost at once."

Cole studied her. How beautiful she was before her sickness took a grip of her, turned her inside out, and bent her over, a lovely rose shrivelled into a brown withered shadow of what it once was.

"What did you do?" she asked suddenly, catching Cole off guard. "When she smiled at you, what did you do?"

"Whoa, Ma, what do you think I did? I ran outside!"

"Oh Reuben, how silly you are. If a young lady of standing smiles, you return it. You bow your head and you bid her good morning, compliment her, and ask her how she is. If you like her, you have to ensure she notices you. And you did like her, didn't you?"

"Why, Ma, she was the most beautiful girl I've ever seen."

"And how will she remember you? As the stupid, awkward boy who ran away like a frightened rabbit? You'll have to go back into town and find her again, Reuben. Don't waste the opportunity. Trust me, life is too short."

Blinking his eyes back to the present, Cole swung his legs over his bed. He sat like that for a moment, thinking. Since the war began, signing up for the army, guided by Sergeant Burnside to become the man he now was, not once had the thought ever entered his head that he might find a companion. Even someone to walk out with underneath the stars, exchanging niceties. He wasn't sure he knew how to react or what to say but one thing he did know, his mother was wise and her words were full of good advice.

Making his decision, he exchanged his buckskins for a fresh shirt and trousers. He even combed his hair. Leaving his gunbelt behind, he marched back to the quarters of Mrs Winter, head high, eyes straight as if he were on parade. He put aside all his fears and trepidations, went straight to the door and knocked on it again.

This time, it was not the lovely Miss Dryson who answered, but Colonel Mathieson. Taken aback by the sight of the young scout, he was for a moment lost for words. "Cole?" he asked at last. "What are you doing here?"

"Please, sir," said Cole, bringing his heels together. "I wish to speak with Mrs Winter."

"There is nothing you need say to Mrs Winter, Cole. Now return to your—"

"It's all right, Colonel," said a kindly voice. Mrs Winter gently moved Mathieson aside and smiled down at Cole. "You must be Reuben?"

Mathieson gaped and Cole, quickly overcoming his shock, smiled, "Yes, Ma'am. I am. Reuben Cole." He saw her then, hovering close behind Mrs Winter. Miss Dryson. Cole beamed and bowed. "At your service, ma'am."

"Then you'd better come in," said Mrs Winter and waved Cole inside.

Mathieson glared, speechless, and Cole looked at him and smiled.

MRS WINTER

The two army men sat across from each other. Mathieson, his uniform newly pressed, sat with a teacup and saucer in his lap, great big hands swamping the crockery as he stared into the bottom of the cup. Cole, across the room, awkwardly sipped at his tea. It was too hot for his liking on such a day as this and the absence of sugar caused him to screw up his mouth at the tartness of the taste.

"While I was home, we always had sugar," said Mrs Winter, sitting beside Mathieson. She had been crying. That much was obvious, due to the puffiness of her eyes and the dark rings that surrounded them. "But here, well, sweeteners of any kind seem very hard to come by."

"I shall try tomorrow, Mrs Winter," said Miss Dryson who stood next to a large, dark wood dresser pressed against the far wall.

It was a small, cramped room, the furniture taking up almost all the available space. A tiny table sat beneath the only window and upon it was a large oil lamp, not yet lit. It soon would be, however. The afternoon was slowly turning to evening, but the heat continued to rage.

Beyond the window, the hubbub of Fort Nelson throbbed as

it always did, the harsh cry of drovers urging mules and carthorses onward, soldiers marching, the bark of Sergeants. That sound alone must cause so much grief, mused Cole.

Everyone jumped when there came a pounding on the door. The quarters in which the women were staying were small and not particularly well built, and the entire edifice shook as the knocking continued urgently. Miss Dryson stood, gave a curtsy, and went to see who it was. Cole heard a male voice and Miss Dryson returned, a little flushed. "Apologies, Colonel, but there is a soldier at the door, telling me that your presence is required."

Mathieson grunted, put his teacup down with great care and stood. He glared towards Cole. "You can accompany me, if you would, Cole."

"I actually wish to stay here, Colonel, and discuss some details with Mrs Winter."

Mathieson looked as if he were about to fall into a fit. As his face reddened, his fist came up. "Cole, I'm ordering you to—"

"Colonel Mathieson," interrupted Mrs Winter, her voice quiet but determined, "I would very much like Mr Cole to remain. I wish to speak with him also. So, if you don't mind ..."

Miss Dryson, smiling that lovely smile of hers, gestured for Mathieson to leave.

The Colonel hesitated, indignant and livid. "I'll see you later, Cole," he snarled through gritted teeth and left.

A palpable release of tension wafted over the room. Cole sat back and sighed while the two women sat down next to each other, their stares penetrating.

"That was awkward," said Miss Dryson.

"Indeed," said Mrs Winter. "I have to say, the Colonel's manner does not fill me with ... how shall I say it? Confidence?"

"Mrs Winter," said Cole, leaning forward, "I don't wish to press you on matters that may cause you more grief than you are already experiencing, however ..."

"Reuben," said Mrs Winter, "as I said, my husband put a

great deal of credence in your loyalty and your honor. He was a proud man who gave his entire life in service to the army. Although we were never wealthy, his pay not being particularly substantial, our life was comfortable. He never felt the desire to further his career, content to be a non-commissioned officer. After the war began, he fought in the First Battle of Bull Run as it has become known. A most dreadful day."

"One of too many, Mrs Winter."

"Indeed. After that awful rout of our troops, my husband made it his life's work to train those raw militiamen into a credible fighting force. There were many such as he, working diligently to bring the war to a swift conclusion. And now, to end his life this way ..." She broke down. Having bravely fought to keep her emotions in check, the resurrection of her husband's selfless duty proved too much.

Miss Dryson shot an apologetic look at Cole before putting her arm around the older woman beside her, holding her while huge, quaking sobs shook her delicate frame.

Clearing his throat, Cole stood up. "I've outstayed my welcome. I'm sorry if I—"

"No," snapped Mrs Winter from behind the sodden lace handkerchief pressed against her eyes. "Please stay, Reuben. I have something else to say." She sniffed loudly and nodded towards Miss Dryson. "I'm all right, Penelope."

Miss Dryson allowed her arm to slide from Mrs Winter's shoulders.

Cole sat down again and waited.

"I cannot accept," Mrs Winter continued, dabbing her eyes, "that my husband, being the man that he was, would have taken his own life. For him to put that noose around his neck and ..." She broke off and, for a moment, Cole thought she would collapse into grief once more. But, gathering herself, she controlled her emotions sufficiently enough to force a smile. "No, Reuben, I cannot accept that."

"Mrs Winter," said Cole, "neither do I."

Both women looked at him, eyes wide with surprise.

"You mean ...?"

"I *mean*, Mrs Winter, I believe your husband was murdered and I intend to discover why and who the perpetrators are."

Back in his bunkhouse, after he lit the single oil lamp, Cole sat and put together what Mrs Winter had told him. The Sergeant had given no indication through personal letters of any reason why he should take his own life. Indeed, the last letter, sent only a fortnight before, included details of the arrangements he had made for her to visit him. He even talked about seeking another post closer to their home. In other words, he was looking to the future. Hardly the aspirations of a man contemplating suicide.

Cole stood up and went across to his side table where he had left his gunbelt.

It was not there.

He stood rooted, going through his actions before leaving the bunkhouse to visit Mrs Winter. He remembered as clear as the day itself that he left his gunbelt right there.

The door creaked open and Cole spun. In the doorway, a black shadow against the rapidly darkening sky without, stood a tall angular individual. The flare of a match as he lit a cigarette illuminated his face: Johnson, the leading rascal in the group that had taunted Cole before he set off to apprehend Shapiro.

"Evening Cole."

"What do you want, Johnson?"

"Come to have a little talk." He chuckled to himself and stepped aside to allow his two sidekicks to push past him. They were big men and seemed to fill the room with their great size.

"What's the matter, Cole? Scared?"

"Go to hell, Johnson."

Johnson sucked in a breath. "My, that's big talk for a man who ain't got his guns. I hear you is real dandy with them firearms, Cole. What might you be like without 'em?"

"What do you want?"

Johnson made a big play in blowing out a long trail of blue-black smoke before he threw the cigarette down and ground it out beneath his boot. "Just come to give you a gentle word of advice."

"And what would that be?"

"Leave Mrs Winter alone."

Cole reeled backwards a little. The words surprised him. "Who's asking?"

"Nobody's asking, Cole. I'm *tellin'* you before you get hurt."

"And if I don't?"

"You know, I thought you'd say that. But even if you hadn't," he chuckled again, "we're still gonna give you a good kickin', Cole. Teach you a long-overdue lesson."

They came at him in a rush, the two big men charging forward, hands outstretched in their eagerness to squeeze Cole's lifeblood out of him.

Sergeant Burnside had organised self-defence lessons for Cole. Ever since, he practiced every day, honing his skills. More than once, he had used what he learned to good effect –

now, even more so.

Using the first man's forward momentum, he turned at the last moment, foot outstretched, and the man rocketed forward, crashing across the side table, splintering it as it collapsed under his weight. Ducking under the second man's tremendous left swing, Cole hit him hard in the solar plexus and struck him across the carotid artery with the edge of his hand, dumping him to the floor. As he straightened to tackle Johnson, the first thug now recovered from his fall, grabbed Cole in a powerful bear-hug, pinning his arms to his side and lifting him off the ground. Johnson moved in, slamming one, two, three punches into Cole's midriff, then delivering a right cross into the young scout's jaw.

The force of the punch sent Cole's senses into a whirl. Another punch into his face did not help him at all and suddenly the room was pitching over his head. This was not good and despite his struggles, the big man's grip was too strong from which to break free. He had enough instinct for survival to throw back his head and crack it into the big man's nose. The man yelped and released Cole from his hug. But Cole was not able to deflect two more punches to his guts from Johnson and another right put him on the floor. Behind him, the big man was bellowing, enraged by the pain he must have been experiencing. A boot struck Cole in the side, throwing him across the room. He landed on his bed, which creaked alarmingly under him.

The big man loomed over him and Cole managed to put the heel of his palm under that ruined nose of his with as much force as he could muster. The big man teetered backwards, lost his balance, and crumpled.

Cole rolled over, winded, confused, unable to find any more strength. Johnson took his chance and rained blows into Cole's ribs, finally ending the fight with a tremendous crack across the scout's jaw, which flattened him onto the bed where he lay, face down and unconscious.

INVESTIGATIONS CONTINUE

He did not know what time it was when he finally came around. Blackness surrounded him and he lay there, waiting for his senses to return. It took several minutes before, dazed, bruised, every muscle throbbing, he rolled over onto his back. Crying out with the effort, he took in several light, quick breaths. Breathing proved difficult and painful. Gingerly, he traced his fingers across his sides. His ribs ached from where Johnson's fists had smashed into them. They could be broken. Trying to sit up, Cole cried out again and flopped back down into the bed. He wouldn't be trying that again for a while.

Johnson had beaten him badly, that much was obvious. Cole had underestimated him. It was not a mistake he would repeat.

He closed his eyes for a moment. When he opened them again it was daylight, the sun trickling through the cracks in the wooden shutters and beneath the main door. Sleep had conquered him, which might not be a bad thing, he mused. Before he attempted to move, he checked his ribs and hissed through clenched teeth. Slowly, he pulled back his shirt, cursing with each movement, craned his neck, and saw the massive bruising covering the right side of his body. Purple and red, the discolored skin was certainly a testament to the power of John-son's fists. Other than that, however, he felt remarkably unscathed. Taking a few breaths, he swung his legs across the bed and sat up.

Pain like a knife's blade stabbed deep into his side. He sat, gasping, waiting for the sensation to slip away. Eventually, it did and, pressing down on the bed, he eased himself to his full height.

He scanned the room. It was a mess, the broken table, shat-tered oil lamp, an old chair in tatters. There was no sign of the big man Cole had floored. They must have taken him outside. Cole wondered if he was dead. No doubt, he said to himself, he would find out soon enough.

Shuffling across to the remnants of a washbasin, he discov-ered sufficient water to splash over his face. Dripping wet, he went to the door and pulled it open.

The harsh sunlight hit him right between the eyes and brought up his forearm to shield himself from the glare. Step-ping onto the parade ground, he became aware of the many stares from the people wandering close by. Soldiers and civilians alike stopped and gawped. He must have looked a dreadful sight.

He wandered over to where the regimental surgeon had his quarters and went straight in. The place was empty, save for the good doctor himself, sitting at his desk, pince-nez perfectly posi-tioned for him to read the broadsheet in his hands. Doc Henson looked up and raised his brows in surprise. "Good Lord. Have you been butted by a buffalo?"

"Kind of. Could you take a look at my ribs, please, Doc? I think they might be busted."

Henson led Cole across to a low-lying couch set against the opposite wall. Without waiting, the doctor pulled apart Cole's shirt and began the examination, his fingers cool as he expertly probed, pressed and penetrated. Cole held his breath at each press of the doctor's fingers.

At last, the examination over, Henson stepped back. "Severely bruised, young man, but not broken. I take it the buffalo got the worse of this encounter?"

Sitting up, Cole rebuttoned his shirt. "Unfortunately no, Doc."

"Well, I think the best bet would be for me to prescribe some simple ointment that you should apply twice a day. It will sting but the effects will not last long and you will soon feel the benefit." Going to a glass-fronted cabinet, Henson delved inside and returned with a small glass bottle. "This is Witch Hazel and it is excellent for drawing out the bruising. Dab it across the welts and within a day, perhaps less, you will be feeling a whole lot better."

Roused awake once again by somebody pounding on his door, Cole rolled out of bed and waited for the pain to subside. Gathering himself on hands and knees, he pushed himself to his feet and shuffled across to the door.

He reeled backwards in surprise to find Miss Dryson standing before him, looking lovely in a pale pastel-blue frock. She wore a broad-brimmed hat with feathers. Hair like golden ringlets sprouted from beneath the brim and fell to her shoulders. She twirled a small but effective parasol, which she closed with a snap as she gasped, "*Reuben!*" She pushed her way inside. "What have they done to you?"

He suddenly realised he had yet to study himself in a mirror. He must have looked a ghastly sight. Self-consciously, he touched the side of his face where the swelling was at its most prominent. "It's nothing."

"*Nothing?* Reuben, you look close to death!" She took charge, guiding him back to his bed while she threw off her bonnet and parasol and went to the washbasin. She groaned. "This is dreadful. Reuben, who has been tending to you?"

Sitting on the edge of his bed, Cole shrugged. "Nobody."

"Well, we'll have to do something about that, won't we?"

She spent the next thirty minutes or so throwing out the old water, replacing it with fresh from a stand-pipe outside. Ignoring the shocked looks of passersby, she returned to Cole's room and set about bathing the cuts and bruises that crisscrossed his face. She worked carefully but quickly, and Cole almost instantly felt better.

He showed her the small bottle of Witch Hazel, which she applied without comment. Cole winced as the ointment stung his flesh but remained quiet, knowing he had to get through this if he was ever to feel remotely human again.

Dipping inside her purse, she produced a small hand mirror. He took it and studied his face. Squeezing shut his eyes, he shook his head and said, "I had no idea how bad I looked."

"You look like one of those Chinese bears I saw once in a zoo back in New York. Big black eyes but none of the cuteness."

She laughed. He gaped. When she laughed a second time, he joined in. The world was returning to normality.

Later, after he dressed in a clean shirt and a pair of army uniform trousers, they walked across the square to where Mrs Winter stayed. Many questioning eyes turned their way. Cole, despite feeling awkward, struggled to prevent his face from warming up. He failed.

"Mrs Winter wishes to speak with you again," explained Miss Dryson. "She meant to tell you the last time you met, but Colonel Mathieson's presence made that impossible. "

They were almost at the entrance when the voice barked out from across the square. Cole sighed loudly and stopped.

Miss Dryson gave him a questioning stare. "What is it, Reuben?" She turned. "Who is that dreadful-looking man?"

Cole, who did not need to turn around to recognise the owner of the loud voice, shook his head. "His name is Johnson. Mathew Johnson. He was one of the men who broke into my quarters and beat me up."

A hand flew to her mouth. "Then we must report him to the Colonel and make—"

"No, Penelope, we leave it alone." He felt her stare and suddenly realised he had called her by her first name. His embarrassment stung him more than Johnson's booming voice. "Apologies, Miss Dryson, I did not mean to be so familiar."

"It's perfectly fine for you to call me Penelope, Reuben. It is, after all, my name." She grinned and he instantly felt better.

"Cole," came Johnson's voice again, "you were told to stay away!"

Slowly, Cole turned. He felt Penelope's hand on his arm but chose to ignore it. Johnson stood there, but this time there was only one thug. Both men appeared incensed. Red-faced and shaking with rage, Johnson took a step forward. Cole immediately went to his hip but then groaned as the absence of his gun flashed into his mind.

Johnson laughed. "Yeah, you're not such a hotshot without your guns are you, Cole? You looking for another beating?"

"Sir," snapped Penelope from nowhere, "I would advise you to withdraw. My mistress, Mrs Winter, is under the personal protection of your Commanding Officer."

The mention of the name Winter certainly had an effect. Johnson stopped dead, his mouth dropping open, nonplussed. "Winter, you say?"

"Yes. Sergeant Winter's widow."

Blinking rapidly, Johnson was lost for words. The big thug beside him leaned over and whispered something in his ear. Head bobbing enthusiastically, Johnson turned away without another word and marched off.

"What was all that about?" asked Penelope.

"I don't know," said Cole cautiously. "I'm not sure if they knew Mrs Winter was here."

"But what has that to do with him?"

Inhaling slowly, Cole shrugged. "I have a feeling I am going to find out soon enough."

. . .

Mrs Winter received Cole with a warm smile, but it was clear to the scout she had been crying again. There was another woman there this time. Prim, straight-backed, she had an aura of authority which Cole immediately picked up on. "This is my good friend, Mrs Lipmann," introduced Mrs Winter.

"I'm pleased to meet you, Mr Cole," said the woman. "I've heard a good deal about you but I must say, I am surprised at how young you are."

"Most soldiers in the army are young, madam," Cole smiled.

"Yes. Unfortunately, I know that all too well. My eldest son was killed at Antietam. My husband I lost only a few months ago in a skirmish. Not even a battle." She shook her head and clasped her hand around Mrs Winter's. "I know the pain of grief all too well, Mr Cole and am here to give my good friend any support she may need."

Penelope, who had been hovering in the corner, now stepped up and whispered something into Mrs Lipmann's ear. The older woman nodded and gathered her things. "I hope we can meet again, Mr Cole. Your assistance in these awful matters is most appreciated."

Cole stood up as the two other women left him alone with Mrs Winter. Clutching his hat on his lap, he sat, and waited.

"I have had some more news, Mr Cole. Bad news, I am afraid. A nice young Lieutenant came to announce, early this morning, that due to the circumstances of my husband's death, he will not receive a military funeral. I had hoped that Colonel Mathieson might use his influence but apparently not. So, it is up to me to arrange for his body to be transported back to our home, where I will lay him to rest in a private plot."

"I'm sorry for all of that, Mrs Winter. Perhaps, if my investigations can continue, I may well be able to clear your husband's name."

"Yes, you said ... but, Mr Cole, by the look of you, these investigations are going to present you with endangerment. I cannot allow you to put yourself in such danger, Mr Cole. Therefore, it would be for the best if we simply resigned ourselves to the fact that my husband's death will never be explained."

"We can't do that, Mrs Winter. With all due respect, I am certain his death is linked to the death of Given Sky, my friend who was brutally murdered. I believe Sergeant Winter was closing in on those responsible and that is why he died."

"We've had this discussion before, Mr Cole and although initially I was in agreement, time has moved rapidly on. I feel we will never find the truth."

At that point, Penelope entered, bearing a silver tray with teapot and cups. "Forgive me, Mistress," she said quietly as she placed the tray on the side table, "but have you told Mr Cole about the letter?"

"Yes, but not the subsequent correspondence," said Mrs Winter patiently. "Reuben, my husband gave me details of a man he had spoken to. You are correct when you say my husband had undertaken investigations into the death of a Native scout. I cannot remember his name but—"

"His name was Given Sky," interjected Cole. "He was my friend."

If Mrs Winter was shocked by this, she gave no indication. Her decorum remained intact. Nodding, she continued. "The man he spoke to is Percival Bryce. He is attached to the supply office, so I understand. Although my husband gave no details of what Mr Bryce had to say, he was certain that it would lead to the eventual solving of the case."

"I will speak with him," said Cole, smiling at Penelope as she handed him a cup of tea. "I do not believe I have ever drunk so much tea since visiting here."

Penelope gave a small curtsy and smiled. "You're welcome, Reuben."

"My husband's ancestry introduced me to tea-drinking," added Mrs Winter. " I've never looked back."

The meeting ended in a much lighter mood than it had begun.

For a moment, as they all sat and drank in silence, something like normality returned. But only briefly. Cole had much to do.

BRYCE

Cole's first stop, on his way to visit Bryce, was the armory. The store, which fronted the warehouse in which numerous weapons and ammunition were kept, was small and dark. Behind the counter, a burly Lance-Corporal was busy checking off items on a printed list. A pencil stub poked out from the corner of his mouth and when Cole came through the door he scowled. "Cole, isn't it?" he asked with no preamble.

Nodding, Cole scanned the shelves that ran the length of the wall behind the counter. Filled with endless boxes of caps, balls, and bags of powder, there were few gaps. "I'm after a Navy Colt, with load."

"Are you, by God?" He chuckled. "Planning on going off on the trail? You'll need a rifle too, I suspect."

"My rifle is at the livery, together with my horse."

"Are you sure about that?"

Cole frowned. "What do you mean?"

"I mean, you should check first, Cole. Rumour has it you received a long-awaited beating, that your rank has been withdrawn and you," his grin grew wider, "are on a short, slippery road to disaster."

Cole tilted his head to the left. "Just give me the goddamned gun."

"Can't do it, Cole. As a civilian, you have no right to bear arms whilst in the confines of the fort." He leaned across the counter. "In other words, get the hell out."

Deciding against further discussion, Cole left, the irksome sound of the Lance-Corporal's laughter setting his teeth on edge. Everyone, apart from Mrs Winter and Penelope, was against him. He already knew that there was a great deal of resentment focused on him, that some did not agree with him being made an army scout at such a young age, and his friendship with the Natives angered many more.

He went to the supply depot, mounting the steps without checking if anyone was close. As his hand wrapped around the door handle, he noticed two men standing some way off. In shirt-sleeve order, they stood under the shade of a poplar tree, arms folded and snarling. Cole sighed and went inside, predicting he would be met with more than scowls when he left.

The place was empty. He went to the counter and rapped on the surface. Nobody arrived, so he took it upon himself to lift the hinged portion of the counter and go through the door at the rear.

He was presented with a large interior divided into rows of storage shelves, unopened crates, boxes, piles of army surplus. He made his way slowly through the various merchandise until he found a round, squat man down on his knees, sorting through an open crate of boots. He did not notice Cole until the scout stepped up behind him and gave a polite cough.

The man jumped and swung around. Aghast, he took in Cole with a quick scan. "Who the hell are you?"

"Name's Cole."

"Cole? Oh my God." He clambered to his feet. "I don't want no trouble," he said as he dusted off the knees to his trousers.

"Trouble? Why should you get trouble from me?"

"I don't know, but you're not a person anyone wants to do business with."

"Are you Bryce?"

The man stopped and took in a trembling breath. "I may be. Why you wanna know?"

"Because I'm here on behalf of Mrs Winter. You know, *Sergeant* Winter's widow? You had a meeting with him, so I understand."

"A meeting?" The man's voice had changed to a high-pitched squawk. His eyes darted around, checking for anyone who might have followed Cole into the store. "I ain't ever had no meeting with anyone. Now, if you don't, I have—"

"Mrs Winter says different. She says the Sergeant had words with you about the death of Given Sky."

"Oh my." Bryce now took to dusting off the green apron he wore. "I don't know what you mean." He went to step passed Cole, but Cole's hand came out to stop him.

"Bryce, let me make it clear. I need to know what you told Sergeant Winter and, after that ..." His eyes roamed the shelving towering over him. "I'd like you to provide me with a gun."

Cole rarely drank. He was nineteen years of age and he convinced himself that he was celebrating his birthday of a month and a half ago. The Fat Belly Saloon was not particularly busy, so he bought himself a small beer with a whisky chaser, found himself a corner table, and sat down to savor his liquor.

Bryce's words reverberated around inside his mind. Once Cole promised the strange little man that nobody else would hear his words, either in a military or civil court, he proved more than forthcoming.

"I heard it from a couple of Indian pals of Given Sky," he told Cole, firing off his words with the rapidity of a Gatling gun. "Seems that Given Sky, he had this girl with him, a squaw by the name of Singing Deer. Her name is fairly self-explanatory and she would often sing over in the Fat Belly Saloon. She was only fifteen. I think Given Sky was her brother, I ain't that sure, but there was nothing untoward between them. This one evening, she was singing in the saloon and these rough types came in. Off-duty beer-swizzlers looking for trouble.

"Anyways, they tried to get all friendly with Singing Deer. Another soldier, name of Lawson, he tried to step in and this big fella, Lance-Corporal Jessop, he floored Lawson with one punch. Broke his jaw. Then Given Sky stepped in. They took him outside and beat the life out of him. Yessir, they beat him to death in the alleyway, covered over the body with all sorts of garbage. A couple of other scouts saw it but they ran off. Nobody wanted to get involved. These men then had their way with Singing Deer. The Indian scouts, they left the fort the next day. I understand they are in Fort Randleson, a broken-down frontier post which is on its last legs. It won't survive the war."

Cole asked further, relevant questions. Bryce reluctantly gave it up for the twenty dollars Cole pressed into his hand. "You promise you won't tell a single soul about what I said?"

Cole said he would honor his promise and now, sitting in the saloon, he felt sick to his stomach about what he'd been told. Without Bryce, he had no witnesses, no proof. He would need to travel across to Fort Randleson as soon as he could. He would need to question the other scouts, talk to Mathieson about Singing Deer, as well as Lawson. Neither might prove to be as forthcoming as Bryce; for Lawson, the shame at being publicly beaten could well work in Cole's favour.

The double batwing doors of the saloon screeched open and Johnson strode in, the big Lance-Corporal close behind, as usual. As soon as he spotted Cole, Johnson's face lit up. "Well, well, if it ain't Mister Cole. See what I did there, pipsqueak? *Mister*? Guess you haven't heard the news, not officially I mean. You've lost your commission, boy. You are no longer a member of the United States Army. Colonel Mathieson has your release papers waiting for you in his office. So, you scoot on over there, pipsqueak, and afterwards, I'll give you another lesson in manners."

He stuck his thumbs in his waistband and went to the bar. Leaning against the counter, the smile never left his face. "Give me a beer, Ned," he said to the barkeep hovering close by. "Another for Tobias here and, oh yeah, nearly forgot, a soda for the boy over there."

Grunting, Ned carried out the order. Johnson handed one beer glass across to his companion, took a large mouthful from his own glass, then sweeping up the bubbling soda, he moved across to where Cole sat. "Here's a little gift for you, pipsqueak." He gently put down the glass of soda in front of Cole. "Hope it ain't too strong for your delicate stomach." He giggled at his joke. "My, you do look in a mess there, Cole. Your face all red and swollen, bit like an over-ripe apple or somesuch. Just imagine what it'll look like when I tan your ass again later."

"You won't do that a second time, Johnson."

"Oh no? And why not?"

"You'll see soon enough." Cole threw back the whisky and stood up.

Johnson's eyes fell on the Colt Navy strapped to Cole's thigh and, shocked, stepped back. "Where the hell you get that?"

"The fact is, Johnson, I've got it. Now, move out of my way. You try to follow me, you'll see how annoyed I can get."

Moving smoothly through the silent saloon, Cole did not look back. He did not need to. He'd stunned Johnson, put him off-balance. A small victory, but one which gave Cole a much-needed boost of satisfaction.

NEWS FROM MATHIESON

There were two sentries outside Colonel Mathieson's office. As Cole approached, one of them advanced, rifle with bayonet pointing directly towards the scout. The second knocked on the door and entered. While Cole waited, hands raised, the second soldier reappeared with Mathieson's adjutant, Lieutenant Owen. "Surrender your revolver, Cole."

"Will I get it back?"

Owen chewed his bottom lip for a moment, "That awaits to be seen."

They escorted Cole into the office and flanked him as, from behind his desk, Mathieson fixed him with a dark stare. "This pains me to say what I'm about to say, Cole."

A thousand different scenarios rushed through Cole's mind. What had he done that had brought him to this situation? As far as he knew, he had not broken any military laws, had not disobeyed orders. His actions during the hunt for Shapiro had brought nothing but praise. So why was Mathieson about to bring down all the furies of Hell upon his head? What could he be facing? Five years? Ten? He shuddered to think.

"You're hardly my favourite person at the moment, Cole. You

have deliberately gone against my wishes and spoken to Mrs Winter. By doing so, you—"

"Begging your pardon, sir, but I did not—"

Mathieson brought his fist down with a tremendous crash on his desk and leaped to his feet. "Damn your eyes, Cole, do not interrupt me!"

Cole brought his heels together in sharp attention.

"The only reason I'm not putting you in chains this very moment is because we have a situation. One that only you are capable of resolving."

Cole frowned, bewildered. He didn't say anything, however. He dared not.

Mathieson pulled in a long, deep breath and calmed himself down. "Shapiro. He's broken out. With the US Marshal only a day away, this is a serious embarrassment to myself. Therefore, you will leave immediately, track him down and bring him back. You leave at once."

"Sir, I'll need a couple of men. Shapiro is a dangerous individual."

"Don't you think I know that?" He flopped into his chair. "I have selected two men to accompany you. Good, resilient and loyal men. Johnson and Weir. They'll be your companions. Now, get your horse saddled up and get to it."

Stunned by what Mathieson had said, Cole slowly saluted and drifted outside as if in a dream. Johnson and Weir? Had the Colonel lost all reason? Or, as Cole believed, was this all a ploy to get rid of him once and for all? Whatever this was all about, Cole had little choice but to comply.

With heavy tread, he made his way to the livery to pick up his horse. Amazingly, his horse was already saddled up, his gunbelt and Navy Colts draped over the saddle and in the leather boot at the front, a Burnside carbine. Cole pulled it free and checked its movement. It was not the Sharps he had used before, the carbine favored by the Sharpshooters, but it was a fine weapon.

Impressed, Cole put it away and looked around for anyone to confirm his acceptance of the equipment. As there was nobody, he led the horse by the reins out towards the parade ground.

He pulled up sharp.

Johnson and Weir, the huge man who had placed him in the bear-hug, were waiting for him astride two shaggy mares. The one supporting Weir appeared decidedly miserable.

"Funny thing fate, ain't it Cole?" Johnson sniggered and popped a cigarette into his mouth. "Let's hope we don't experience any accidents on the way."

"Or on the way back," chuckled Weir.

Ignoring them, Cole mounted up. His horse was in much better condition than his two associates. If the journey proved arduous, this fact could go against the two roughnecks. Only time would tell.

Cole led his horse in silence towards the main gate. He spotted Penelope standing on the boardwalk before Mrs Winter's quarters. She raised her hand slightly and Cole tipped his hat. He mouthed "see you soon" before he kicked his horse into a canter and soon left Fort Nelson behind.

ACROSS THE OPEN PLAINS

They cut across country at an easy amble. Cole scoured the land, looking for signs. The tracks were numerous. Many riders had ridden this way and, as the ground was so dry, the tracks were mingled together. As they neared a small glade beside a dried-up stream, Cole dismounted and examined the nearby vegetation. Here, the scrub was so dry that as he put brown leaves between his fingers, they disintegrated into fine powder.

"It ain't rained for weeks," said Cole to himself. The others sat a little way off, smoking or, in Weir's case, chewing tobacco. "Signs are not easy." He got down on his knees as something caught his eye. "Did Shapiro smoke?"

"How in the hell should I know?" snapped Johnson.

Cole picked up the remnants of a thinly rolled cigarette. "Could be he stopped here for a break before ..." He wandered further amongst the brittle undergrowth and, sure enough, found the signs of a small fire, the charred hunks of wood cold and long dead. "How long ago did he break out?"

"His cell was discovered empty only this morning."

"He was well clear of the fort by then. Two days at least. Wasn't he ever checked?" Cole turned and glared at Johnson.

"Why you asking me? I wasn't his jailer."

"Yeah, but you know more than you are tellin', that's for sure."

"What's that supposed to mean?"

Cole got to his feet. "Nothin'," he said and returned to his horse. He pointed his finger across the endless plain. "He's out there. Could be he has a gun. Interesting that my Sharps rifle was missing from my horse furniture."

Johnson readjusted himself on his horse. "I don't like your tone, Cole. I don't like it at all."

"Seems like you is accusing us of something," added Weir. He leaned to the right and spat out a long trail of brown, stinking tobacco juice.

"You could be right, Tobias." He turned his malevolent gaze towards the scout. "Is that what you is doing, Cole? Accusing us?"

Shaking his head, Cole eased his horse back into a canter. He had no wish to confront these men out here. Not yet at least.

They rode on, Cole setting a steady pace. In the heat, the others soon tired, forever complaining that they needed to rest. Cole, well used to riding for prolonged periods, ignored them, knowing he must do everything he could to overtake Shapiro.

After several hours, he did rest. Not for himself, but for the horse. He would lead it to whatever meager shade he could find, remove the saddle, and wipe the animal down. He fed it oats and gave it whatever water he could.

"What in the hell," said Johnson, riding up to him on the third of these short stops. He was washed in sweat, his face drawn, lips cracked.

Cole gave him a disgusted look. The man's water canteens were empty. Weir, coming up next to him, was in a worse condition. He threw himself down under the shade of some withered trees, leaves long since gone, and lay there, panting like a distressed dog.

"How long we been on this trail?" demanded Johnson, dismounting.

"About six or so hours," said Cole, glancing skywards. "We have to continue, overtake him as soon as we can."

"We have to get some sleep," said Johnson, staggering around like a drunkard. "And I have no water, damn it. I *need* water."

"You should always conserve water as best you can."

"What the hell are you, my nursemaid? You think I don't know how to look after myself out here, boy?"

Cole shrugged and did not reply. He was past caring about these two. If they chose to squander their limited resources, then so be it. "I will scout ahead, try and find some water. It won't be easy."

"You can't leave us," said Johnson becoming angry. His hand hovered close to his gun.

"If I don't find you water, you'll die."

"You have enough water, damn your eyes! Share it with us."

"I have only enough for myself. I'll find more, then come back. We can then refill our canteens, water the horses, and move on. I won't be but an hour." He swept his hand across the view. "There is water here. You just need to know where to look."

"You better come back ..."

"What's that? A threat? Don't you trust a little pipsqueak like me?"

Johnson looked as if he were about to draw his gun. For a moment everything stopped and Cole, sensing the rising tension, readied himself.

"Damn it!" spat Johnson, relaxed his gun hand and flopped down in the dirt. "Be quick, that's all. Damned quick."

Cole took an easy gait, not wishing to exert his horse any more than was necessary. He found the trees hanging over a virtually dry riverbed and knew this was the spot. As he led his horse down to the remaining puddles and let her drink, he refilled his canteens. He would return to the camp, bring them both here and ...

His experienced eyes scanned the ground as he thought things through. The tracks here were easy to read. A single horse and rider, stopping for water and then, instead of moving on, turning back. Back the way they had come.

"Ah shit," he spat and quickly readied his horse and mounted up.

Shapiro had doubled back after no doubt watching them for some time, making his plans, waiting for the right opportunity to strike. And now Cole had left those two numbskulls back in the camp. What a fool he had been!

As he hauled himself into the saddle, the sound of distant gunshots came to him. Without another thought, he kicked his horse into a frantic gallop.

He was too late.

They were both dead – Johnson, propped against a tree, lifeless eyes staring into the distance, Weir lying on his back beside him. It looked as if Johnson had been shot at close range while Weir's throat gaped open horribly where Shapiro's blade sliced open his larynx.

Slowly drawing his gun, Cole scanned the immediate surroundings, searching for any signs. He carefully led his horse across to where the others had tied theirs to a nearby tree. He quickly checked the animals. They seemed fine. A little thirsty perhaps, but otherwise remarkably fit.

However, there was something not right. Cole looked again, concentrating on outcrops of rocks and patches of parched tinder-dry scrub. His eyes wandered over the ground. Someone had recently walked through here. Whoever it was had walked on foot, tread measured and slow. No doubt it was Shapiro. He had come upon the others as silently as a breeze. Well versed in surprise tactics, the former bushwhacker would have had little problem approaching the men undisturbed.

Like now.

Cole sensed rather than heard the approach of someone. He groaned and look across to his left. Shapiro stood there, broad grin on his sunbaked face. And in his hands, Johnson's old cavalry carbine.

Cole, the fury churning around inside him, cursed his stupidity.

"Drop your gun," said Shapiro, "before I blow a hole in you wider than a canyon."

The Navy fell to the ground and Cole stepped back.

"Now, you tell me how many more are on my tail."

Frowning, Cole shrugged. "We is the only three."

"Nah," said Shapiro, easing back the hammer of the carbine. "I seen him. He thought he was mighty clever, keeping his distance, but I seen him. There'll be others too, so tell me and no more lies. How many others are—"

Shapiro's head exploded like an over-ripe fruit, almost immediately followed by a tremendous boom. Cole threw himself to the ground, gathering up the Navy and rolling across to take cover. He lay there, head down, breathing hard.

He recognised the retort of that rifle. It was a Sharps. Someone out there was a trained Sharpshooter and now they were taking a bead on Cole.

RETURN TO NELSON

Rooted to the spot, Cole closed his eyes and waited for the inevitable bringing down of the curtain. After several moments, he realized this wasn't about to happen, and opened his eyes. He looked around slowly. There was no one. He reminded himself, as if he needed reminding, that he had made a similar mistake with Shapiro. Slowly, he dipped down and picked up the Navy Colt. He dropped it back into the holster.

The voice called out across the open landscape. "Cole, I want you to get back on your horse and ride the hell out. I ain't gonna kill you, Cole, despite me wanting to. If you come after me though, I will. You won't see it coming. I have a bead on you right now and I can shoot out your eye from a thousand yards. You go back to Nelson and you can investigate the death of your miserable friend. It wasn't me who killed him, I tell you that much, and as for Sergeant Winter, well, he just asked a few too many questions."

Lifting his head, Cole shouted, "You think I believe any of that? It's you, Fraser isn't it? You're no Indian lover and if you had had the chance to kill Given Sky, you would have done so."

"Sure, I hated him, like I hate all of those murderin' heathens, but I wasn't the driver in this. It was Johnson, Cole. Johnson killed him. Mathieson knew it. He and Johnson they came to an arrangement because Mathieson hated that Indian also. Not because he was an Indian but simply because Mathieson despises anyone who is different. Johnson has something on Mathieson I think because, otherwise, the Colonel would have thrown Johnson to the wolves. In the US Army, murder is murder and needs to be investigated ... but nothing happened. No questions were ever asked and nobody paid for it. None of us, especially not Mathieson."

"Why would the Colonel get himself involved in a murder?"

"Like I say, there was something *deep* going on and Johnson knew what it was. I guess that if Mathieson threatened him, then Johnson would let the whole world know what that secret was. If all that is true, then the good Colonel has someone protecting him." An eerie chuckle. "I should say *was* protecting him. Mathieson is all undone. You find out what the secret was, Cole, and you'll find out who had Winter killed."

"So, you know that what happened to Winter was no suicide?"

Again that horrible chuckle. "Just go on back to Nelson, Cole. You'll find all your answers there. Mathieson, he is doing everything to protect his own hide. Why you think he sent you out here with Johnson?"

Cole shook his head, hoping what he thought was the answer might prove to be wrong. Fraser's next few words, however, proved those fears to be true.

"Yeah, that's it, squirt. Mathieson hoped you would end up killing Johnson before you too was killed. All of that was done for you, thanks to that renegade fella who was about to take you out."

"You mean Shapiro?"

"Yeah. A snarled-up sonofabitch if ever there was one. You know his cell door was probably left unlocked the night he escaped? That's my take on it and I reckon I know who did it in the hope that you'd all kill each other. Mathieson. His plan almost worked."

"Why did you help? Why didn't you just do as Mathieson hoped for? That we'd kill one another?"

Fraser shrugged. "I'm heading down to Mexico and you'll never see me again. I don't want to be looking over my shoulder for the rest of my life. I reckon if you go back and discover the truth for yourself, they'll put Mathieson in prison for the rest of his life."

"And why wouldn't I come and hunt you down for your part in this?"

"I'm betting you won't. You're a decent soul, Cole; you want justice. But bringing me to face trial, that won't bring any justice. What's done is done. Best leave it be because Mathieson, he's the mastermind behind all this. He's the one, not me. I went along with it true enough, but I'm hoping the fact that I saved your life will sort of balance the books."

All went quiet. Cole waited, straining to hear. But Fraser was good. His years of serving with the Sharpshooters had taught him how to remain hidden, how to approach silently, shoot from a distance. It was only when the sound of pounding horse hooves reached him that Cole relaxed. Fraser had ridden off and all Cole had to do was mount up and return to Nelson.

He decided against it.

Nothing could shake the images rolling around inside his head. Given Sky was his friend, one of the few in Fort Nelson who spent time with him, regaled stories of frontier life, showed him new aspects of tracking Cole had not yet unearthed for himself.

"When a man rides," Given Sky said one evening as they sat outside the tepees the Indian scouts set up for themselves, "he does not look. I mean, really *look*. He sees the ground, the way it changes, from rolling pasture to blighted scrub. He sees that but he does not think to look and ask the question why. Turn your eyes to the sky.

Read the signs for how the weather will change. Know when rain will come, storms, and in the winter months the snow. All of these things are written for us to discover. You, my young friend, you must search out and understand the signs. You must make this your life's work. Only then can you think of yourself as a scout."

They often rode out together across the plains and, every so often, Given Sky reined in his pinto, got down, and showed Cole the signs. Cole was good, amongst the best, and he could read the land as well as any Native. Given Sky, however, he went beyond the signs. It was almost as if he becaame part of the land itself, an intimate companion, and knew all its secrets.

Throughout long summer evenings, Singing Deer would lift her voice and melt all their hearts. Whenever he listened to those plaintiff renditions of traditional laments, his heart soared. Closing his eyes, he'd lie back and allow her voice to carry him into another existence where only peace and beauty lived. He wished for those moments to last forever.

And now ... they were both gone. His friends also. And Fraser was responsible.

It took him less than three hours to come across Fraser. He had ridden hard and made no attempt to disguise his tracks, convinced Cole would not follow him. Now, there he was, sitting next to his campfire, preparing something to eat as if he did not have a care in the world, his arrogance galling. At that moment, Cole hated him more than anyone else he had ever met. Here was the man responsible for the deaths of so many innocents. Justice *must* be served.

Forcing himself to simmer the anger bubbling within, he drew his carbine and checked the load. Leaving his horse in a secluded glade, Cole wriggled forward on his belly until he reached a vantage point overlooking Fraser's camp. There he was, munching his supper, oblivious.

Cole took aim with the Burnside. It may not have had the range of the Sharps, but it was a good weapon nevertheless.

He thought of Given Sky and Singing Deer, how they had had their entire lives ahead of them. And how Sergeant Winter had shrugged off danger and did his best to unmask their killers.He thought of Whitefoot's death and how Fraser had tried to put the blame of the old Indian's death on him. He swallowed down the anger,the hate and, drawing in a deep breath, he settled himself and shot Fraser through the head.

Standing up, he looked down to where the dead ex-Sharpshooter lay. He would not have felt the bullet that ended his life. There would have been no suffering. It was an uneven comparison to what Given Sky must have gone through.

Blowing out a loud sigh, Cole went down to Fraser's camp, unstrapped the horse's saddle and struck its rump with his hat, sending it running off across the sparse land. He then checked Fraser and stood looking down at the corpse. He felt no elation at the death of the murderer, only an empty, sick feeling laced with regret. Why did men do the most awful things to others, he wondered. When would there ever be a time when people could live side-by-side, in acceptance and peace? He doubted he would ever live to see such a thing and this depressing thought settled in his stomach and spread. Deflated, he took the dead man's Sharps and returned to his horse.

Later, gathering the other horses back at his camp, Cole threw Shapiro's corpse across the back of one of the animals. There could be a reward for the return of the renegade. Perhaps there then would be some good to have come out of this whole ghastly affair. He struck out in the direction of Fort Nelson. He felt no satisfaction at having avenged Given Sky's murder. There was still work to do.

It was the evening of the second day when Cole rode into Fort Nelson. The place was much as he'd left it, although a little quieter now that dusk was falling. He went across to the doctor's surgery and knocked on the door. A light showed from inside and directly the door opened.

Doc Henson stood holding a large oil lamp. He was dressed for bed and wore a long nightgown which reached the floor. His hair appeared a tussled mess and he stifled a yawn. "Cole? Is that you? What's happened? Are you hurt?"

"No, nothing like that, Doc. I just need you to keep something for me." He handed over a neatly folded bundle of papers. "I've written everything down. Doc. It'll be disputed if it ever gets to court, but it's truthful, every word of it."

"What are you talking about?" Henson took the papers. "Is this a confession?"

"No. It's the story of who killed Given Sky. It was told to me by Fraser, the Sharpshooter. I still have a number of pieces to fit together, but the bulk of it is there. If anything happens to me, Doc, pass it on to the US Marshal's office."

"If anything happens to you? Cole, you're frightening me with all of this."

"Please, Doc." Cole reached across and squeezed Henson's forearm. "All being well, I'll come through all this unscathed but in case I don't ..." He smiled and waited as Henson weighed up the options.

"All right," said Henson at last. "I'll keep this but only until you come back. That's something I'm depending on you doing, Cole."

Relieved, Cole bade Henson goodnight before leading his horse to the hitching rail outside the Commanding Officer's quarters. He looped the reins around the hitching rail and mounted the steps. The sentry there stopped him and Cole sighed. He turned to find a small gathering of inquisitive people collected around the horse that bore Shapiro's body. They were muttering amongst themselves in subdued awe.

"Wait here," said the sentry and knocked on the door before going inside.

Cole waited, leaning over the balustrade in front of Mathieson's office. He did not return the open stares of the bystanders. Instead, kicking his heels, he gazed down to the ground and waited in silence. As soon as he was finished with Mathieson, he promised himself a visit to Penelope.

"The Colonel will see you now," announced the sentry.

Cole found Mathieson sitting at his desk, uniform tunic pulled open, hands across his paunch, fingers interlaced. He stared into the distance, lost in thought. Cole stood and looked. The Colonel did not respond and for one awful moment, Cole thought he was dead. He cleared his throat, "Er, Colonel, sir, I have returned with Shapiro. He's dead."

Mathieson raised his head. Blinking rapidly, it took several moments for him to realise Cole was standing there. "Cole? Cole …" He stood up. Shaking, he leaned across his desk, palms flat on the top, and took several deep, labored breaths. "There's … Cole, sit down."

A lump developed in Cole's throat. He reached for the nearby chair and drew it closer. "Colonel, has something happened? I have brought Shapiro in and—"

"Shapiro?" He shook his head. "Cole, did you … did you discover anything about …" A shaking hand ran over his face. "Damn it, Cole, all of this … it's too much, damn you. Too much."

Frowning, Cole leaned forward. "I'm not sure what you mean, sir, when you say 'discover anything'?"

"What happened to the others, Cole? Johnson? Where is he?"

"He's dead."

Mathieson's jaw dropped. "Oh my God … was it Shapiro?"

"He bushwhacked them while I was out on the range looking for tracks. He lured us into a trap … but that's not the worst of it. Fraser, the Sharpshooter? He was the one who killed Shapiro. Then, he told me some things, Colonel, *extremely* disturbing things."

"Ah ... yes. He told you I was mixed up in the murder of that Indian, didn't he?" Mathieson's face grew hard and, with his eyes narrowing into slits, he sat down again, his eyes boring into Cole. "Tell me everything, boy. And I mean *everything*."

Releasing a long breath, Cole retold the entire story as relayed to him by Fraser. Mathieson listened in silence, his expression grave but, other than that, he did not flinch or respond in any way. When Cole came to the end of the story, Mathieson pulled out a cigar from a box on his desk, cut off the end, and lit it. Reclining in his chair, he surveyed the ceiling and silently puffed on his smoke. "That's quite a story," he said at long last. "You believe it?"

"Fraser told me thinking I would not react against him as, so he reminded me, he had saved my life."

"And so ... what have you done with him?"

"I let him go," lied Cole. He studied Mathieson's face. There was the slightest relaxing of his eyes. "He told me he was riding down to Mexico so nobody need know anything about what he said."

"Question still stands, Cole. You believe what he said?"

"With your involvement in the death of Given Sky?" Cole spread out his hands. "I don't know what to think. I'm not sure why you, as Commanding Officer of this fort, would protect a known murderer like Johnson. You knew he and his cronies beat up and killed Given Sky and yet you did nothing. And then there is the apparent suicide of Sergeant Winter. He didn't kill himself, did he, Colonel?"

Mathieson held Cole's stare without blinking. He blew out a long stream of smoke. "You have no proof, have you, of my involvement?"

"Other than Fraser's word? No. But I think I can find out, Colonel. I mean to meet with Mrs Winter and see if anyone has spoken to her. I believe someone has."

"You've already been snooping around, Cole. I think you need to give up on this."

"Not until I learn the truth."

"Well, I'm sorry to say, you won't be getting that truth from Mrs Winter." He stood up again and went to the far corner of his office. There was a painting on the wall, a mountain scene, soaring peaks topped with snow. In the foreground, a lake. Mathieson tapped the frame with his cigar. "This was my wife's. She came from Germany. Bavaria. We met many years ago, before the Mexican War. She was working in the government administration offices over in Illinois."

He shook his head and sniffed loudly. "We were married after what you might call a whirlwind romance and she accompanied me on my first posting as a spotty Second-Lieutenant just outside Kansas City. It was a rat's nest of a fort but we were happy, Cole. Can you believe that? *Me*, being happy?" He turned around and Cole was shocked to see a single tear rolling slowly down the man's cheek. "She contracted measles. Don't ask me how. Maybe it was the fetid air of the west. Who knows? Fact is, she died, and I don't think I have ever got over it."

"I'm sorry to hear that, Colonel. Life out here is pretty unforgiving."

"One day you can tell me your story, Cole. I'm sure you have one, despite you being so young." He grinned.

The action brought a tremor of fear to Cole's insides.

"Mrs Winter and her companion, Miss Dryson, they left the Fort some days ago."

"They left? Where did they go?"

"Back east. Mrs Winter has accepted that her husband took his own life."

"But that's not true! She told me she did not believe—"

"She was persuaded, Cole, that the best course of action was to accept my findings. Sergeant Winter took his own life. That was what my official report states and that's the end of the matter. As such, he would not receive a military funeral and his pension would not go to her. We take scandals such as this extremely seriously, Cole. He disgraced his regiment."

"But it's all lies, Colonel. You know it is!" Cole stood up. "I shall visit her, make her see sense. We have witnesses about what happened to Given Sky and I am certain it is all tied in with Singing Deer. Winter must have come to the same conclusion and he paid for that with his life." He glared towards his Commanding Officer. "No, Colonel. This is not the end of the matter. I mean to find out what happened and the depth of your involvement. And if you try to stop me, be warned that I am not a pushover. Ask Johnson if you don't believe me."

"You killed Johnson, didn't you, Cole? You murdered him in cold blood."

"Shapiro did that, Colonel. Then Fraser shot him."

"But again you have no proof. So, it's your word against Fraser's. And oh," the Colonel threw up his arms, "Fraser isn't here to tell us the truth. He's gone to Mexico. Convenient. For you."

"I'll find the rest of the proof I need, Colonel. I have others that will tell me. This whole situation stinks and I believe it all hinges on what happened to Singing Deer."

Mathieson strode forward dangerously, his face thunderous, and he gripped Cole around the throat. "My advice, you snivelling little wretch, is to go back to your bunk and keep your nose out of this. I know that you went to see Bryce. Let me tell you, that idiot won't confirm any of it, you hear me? Nothing is going to stand up in court, Cole, none of it. So, you go about your duties because if you don't, then you might just suffer an accident." He released his grip and pushed Cole away. "Now get out, Cole. And watch your back."

REVELATIONS

Standing outside Mrs Winter's quarters, Cole gently rapped on the door, then repeated the action hoping against hope he would receive an answer. He did not and, head held low, he turned.

"Mr Cole, how are you?"

It was Mrs Lipmann. She had come upon the young scout so quietly, he did not notice her approach until she spoke. He grinned. "You'd make a good scout, Mrs Lipmann. You have the knack of moving as quietly as a ghost!"

"I do hope not, Mr Cole but I think you did not hear me because you are somewhere else."

Frowning, Cole tilted his head. "Somewhere else?"

"Yes. Please, this will explain." She produced a rolled-up piece of paper and handed it over. "That is from Penelope. She, together with Mrs Winter, left the fort a few days ago. It was a sad day. I had grown close to them both, shared in their grief." She stepped forward and took Cole by the elbow. "We must speak you and I, Mr Cole. Please join me for coffee.

A little time later, they sat in the quiet confines of the only coffeehouse in the fort. Although holding well over two thousand men, coffee was not their drink of choice when they were off duty. There were two other customers sitting in the corner. They were junior officers, but they were well out of earshot.

Nevertheless, as she spoke, Mrs Lipmann kept her voice low. "I understand you went to see Mr Bryce, at the supply store?"

"How did you know that?"

"Because he is a good friend and he came to see me to tell me." She sipped her coffee. "Not everyone in this place is corrupt, nor are they without honour. Mr Bryce has suffered a good deal since Sergeant Winter's passing."

"He told me about what happened at the Fat Belly saloon the night Given Sky was murdered."

"Yes. You should speak with Private Lawson, Mr Cole. He has information but has kept it to himself. He has already been demoted. He was a Corporal, you know."

"I did not know."

"Now, he spends most of his time cleaning out latrines. He lives in fear of his life, Mr Cole so he may not be all that forthcoming with his information."

"How do you know all this, Mrs Lipmann?"

"My late husband was well liked and well respected, Mr Cole. Many of the men who served with him mourned grievously when he was killed. The attendance at his funeral was quite incredible. Many of those men knew that my husband would have wanted truth to prevail. They spoke to me of many things." Her voice broke a little as she faltered in the regaling of her tale. "You must be careful, Mr Cole. The Colonel, he has a long reach."

"The Colonel? So, it's true. He *is* involved in all of this?"

She looked around, making sure that the two officers were indeed unable to hear. She leaned forward and beckoned for Cole to do the same. "I know what the Colonel did. Only because Private Lawson and others told me. Despite my pleas, Lawson refused to give any form of testimony so Mathieson remains unpunished. I am only telling you now because I know I can trust you."

"Of course, you can, Mrs Lipmann. But ... what is it that

Mathieson did? I know Johnson had some control over him. I also know that Mathieson sent me out to find Shapiro with Johnson in the hope that I would kill him."

"That strikes me as being something the Colonel would most certainly wish for." She finished her coffee, set the cup down on its saucer, and turned it in her hands. "Colonel Mathieson took more than a shine to Singing Deer. He forced himself upon her." She closed his eyes. "More than once. He moved her into his private quarters, making her a sort of concubine. Given Sky discovered the truth and ... well, the rest is history, so they say."

Cole listened, appalled. He sat back and wanted to speak but his throat, closed and dry, prevented him. He swilled down the last of his coffee, now cold. "I had no idea."

"Nobody speaks of it. Nobody dares, Mr Cole. When she heard of Given Sky's death, Singing Deer took her own life. Mathieson was devastated, despite it all being his fault. He'd ordered Johnson and Jessop to kill the scout, you see. That was the hold Johnson had over him."

"If I can persuade Lawson and Bryce to testify, we could put Mathieson away. In fact, he would probably face the hangman's noose."

"You would have to give those poor men guarantees, Mr Cole. I doubt you could do that." She held his stare.

What lay behind those eyes, he wondered. Something unsaid, something she *dared* not say. Was she asking him, urging him to take the law into his own hands? He cleared his throat. "I'm not an assassin, Mrs Lipmann. I can only hope the law dictates what happens to Mathieson. Despite his guilt, that could prove almost impossible even if I could get those guarantees you mention. But I will try."

DECISIONS

C ole had yet to unpack properly. He made his way to his bunkhouse. Once he had shared this plain, uninspiring room with the other Indian scouts. Since their move to Fort Randleson, the place was eerily quiet. He had his cot, under which he kept a small trunk and a washstand with an accompanying washbasin and jug. Three other bunks were arranged across the opposite wall. Other than those few meager pieces of furniture, there was nothing to break up the overriding sense of loneliness which seemed to seep out of the very woodwork.

Throwing himself down on the thin mattress, Cole put his hands behind his head and stared at the ceiling. The impossibility of his task lay before him and consumed every thought. To not only clear Sergeant Winter, but also bring to justice Mathieson and the others responsible for the deaths of Given Sky and Singing Deer. Perhaps Lawson could help. If only Cole had something to use leverage with, one of those guarantees Mrs Lipmann spoke of. He breathed a long sigh and closed his eyes.

He had no way of telling for how long he slept. Exhaustion overwhelmed him but when the door to his quarters creaked open and threw the insipid light of evening into the room, he was instantly awake. Without waiting, he rolled out of his bunk and reached for his gun just as the big shape loomed over him. Groggy, only half-awake, Cole barely managed to bring up his arm and block the swinging blow aimed at his head. It was enough to prevent the fist from cracking into his jaw, but not enough to cushion the sheer power of the punch.

His arm rang with the pain that shot through it. Crying out, Cole threw himself backwards and went into a half-crouch. The murkiness of the room offered him little protection and he now had only one functioning arm. His left throbbed and hung useless. With his right, he drew his pistol, the sound of the hammer being cocked sounding impossibly loud in that enclosed space.

The huge bulk of a man in front of him retreated a step. Cole clambered to his feet. His arm hurt like sin and he shook it in a vain attempt to bring some life back to the tendons. "Don't move an inch," he snarled.

From the doorway, another figure cackled. Cole took a chance and shot a glance in the direction of the doorway. There was no mistaking the cavalry carbine in the second assailant's hands. "Drop your piece, Cole."

Cole had no plans of surrendering. He had too many questions to ask. In a flash, he dove behind his cot and threw it on its side just as the carbine went off. It was an old mussel-loader and Cole knew he had enough time to make his own shots count. As the man at the doorway span around, Cole shot him high up on the shoulder, turned and put three into the big attacker who was moving in for the kill. He crashed face down across the edge of the cot, rolled over onto his back, and remained still.

Not waiting for the next attack, Cole moved across the bunkhouse to the wounded man lying half-in, half-out of the room, groaning and bleating, "You've done killed me, Cole."

"No I ain't," said the scout and turned the man over to face him. "Not yet anyways." Easing back the hammer of his Navy, he put the end of the barrel into the man's mouth. "Now, you're gonna tell me who sent you and why."

. . .

Lieutenant Owen and Doc Henson stood in the bunkhouse. The doctor, summoned by one of the soldiers who arrived to investigate the gunfire, read through the testimony given by the man Cole had shot. It detailed everything and Owen, who listened in disbelief at the words, sat at one point, put his head in his hands, and struggled to find any words to explain how he felt.

"Once you match that with what Bryce and Lawson have to add," said Cole, who busied himself cleaning and reloading his Navy Colt, "I don't think there will be any doubt as to Mathieson's guilt."

Owen looked up at last. "I will send a telegram across to the US Marshal's office in Kansas City. It will take whoever they send a few days to reach us. Until then, we shall have to put the Colonel into a cell." The Lieutenant put on a pained expression. "I'm not relishing the idea of doing that, I must admit."

"We have no choice," said Cole, standing up. "I'll ride over to his private quarters. I think it best coming from me that he is under arrest."

Owen could not disguise the look of relief falling over his features. "He may not come quietly, Cole. You should take care."

"I'm sick of taking care, Lieutenant. Mathieson sent men to kill me. I told Mrs Lipmann I am not an assassin. I think I may have changed my mind."

He went to move past the two men but Doc Henson caught his arm. "You must not let your heart rule your head, Reuben. The Colonel is a murderer and should be brought to justice."

"Thanks, Doc. I'll remember that." And with that, he left.

COLONEL MATHIESON

The lonely building, standing a mile or so from Fort Nelson, was a well-built and beautifully rendered single-story twin-fronted cabin. On the right wall, a brick-built chimney stack, to the front, a pair of bay windows flanked the main door. Steps led up to this entrance, a white painted fence enclosing the entire property. It appeared, at first sight, to be the perfect place to spend one's time, a homey, comfortable residence well-suited for a Commanding Officer. This was Mathieson's retreat, a place where he could relax and wind away the hours and try to forget the rigors of his responsible position: Commander of Fort Nelson, one of the most important and strategically placed forts in the entire Union Army.

Except that Mathieson was a murderer and defiler of Singing Deer.

Sitting astride his horse, Cole studied the building, remembering Given Sky, the times they had spent together. He never met Singing Deer but felt somehow that she was a kind, talented young girl, plucked from this world by the avarice and cruel perversions of Mathieson. Cole, declaring to Mrs Lipmann that he was not an assassin, had come to terms with the idea that perhaps he was. Circumstances worked away at his sense of justice. The courts might find Mathieson guilty, they might not. Cole could not take that chance.

He checked his Navy Colt and eased himself out of the saddle. Leading his horse across the open approach to the house, he tied the horse's reins around one of the fence rails. He checked all around him. It was not beyond the bounds of possibility that Mathieson could have set himself up amongst nearby rocks or scrub and was, at that very moment, aiming at Cole's back.

Somehow, Cole doubted it.

He carefully went up the steps, senses alert. There were no sounds from within. Icy fingers played around the nape of his neck. Drawing in a breath, he tried the handle and found it to be open. He pressed it down and eased the door open.

A small hallway presented itself. An open door to the left and to the right, two more doors. Ahead, another room, possibly a dining room or kitchen.

He put his head around the door to his left. It was a plainly decorated sitting room, armchair placed in front of the empty fireplace. Bookcases filled with leatherbound volumes lined the walls together with paintings hanging between the gaps, not too dissimilar to the one in the Colonel's quarters back in the fort. This would be where Mathieson spent his evenings.

Cole stepped back into the hallway. He eased back the hammer to his Navy. Something was not right. If Mathieson had returned here, there were no signs. The atmosphere spoke of unhurried order, immaculately presented, and as clean as a Southern Gentleman's plantation home down in Alabama.

He paused outside the first of the closed doors and put his ear to the woodwork. No sounds. Sucking in another breath, he pushed open the door and stepped inside.

This was Mathieson's office. More books along the wall, more paintings, a desk with a large bay window behind it, a single oil lamp, not lit, an inkwell with a pen next to it.

And Mathieson.

Upper body slumped across the desk, right hand still clutching his Colt Paterson, the blood blooming around his obliterated head.

Suicide. The coward's way out. At least for Mathieson.

Cole slumped into a nearby chair, sat and stared. He felt cheated. He felt everyone was cheated. Mathieson would not face the ignominy of a trial, the shame, the scandal. He had escaped everything and justice had not been served.

Soldiers came some hours later. Together with Lieutenant Owen, they found Cole sitting in the exact same position, in a sort of trance, lost to the world. Owen gently relieved Cole of his Navy, sniffed at the barrel and shook his head towards the others. He then crossed to Mathieson, pressed his fingers against the side of the Colonel's neck and waited, eyes closed, concentrating hard. He already knew what the outcome would be but he needed this absolute verification.

After several seconds, he straightened up and his eyes fell on the note, neatly folded on the desk. He picked it up, opened it, and read the hastily scratched words.

For those who find me here, let me, first of all, say I make no apologies for taking my own life. I had little choice. As the weight of evidence built up everywhere this was the only course left open to me.

It is true, I did find myself drawn to Singing Deer. I swear, I did my very best to resist her but I failed and for that I am sorry. She was a lovely young woman and I took from her everything she ever was. Her brother, the scout Given Sky, discovered what had happened and he threatened to kill me. I paid Johnson, Jessop and Weir to murder him. Later, Sergeant Winter unearthed everything so I fabricated his death, making it look like suicide. Winter was a first-class soldier, a man of honor and duty. I wish the records to show his true worth and to exonerate him. Please give his widow, Mrs Winter, my sincerest apologies for causing so much suffering.

I hope that, in time, my period as commander of Fort Nelson will show I was a man who worked with due diligence to ensure the eventual victory of our forces. I always strived to do the right thing, except in this one instance.

Signed, Colonel Mathieson, Commander-in-Chief, Fort Nelson, 1863.

Owen refolded the letter. He did not speak. Turning, he gestured for the other soldiers to help Cole to his feet.

"Put him on his horse and ride back to the fort. Inform Doctor Henson what has occurred here." He sighed heavily. "I will wait for his arrival."

The two soldiers saluted and gently lifted Cole to his feet. One of them eased the Navy from the scout's grip and slid it into its holster. Then they left, Cole's eyes unfocused, dull, almost lifeless.

Owen watched them leave, then sat down in the chair Cole recently occupied and read through the letter one more time.

"What a mess," he said to himself and then, like Cole, he seemed to drift away, heart heavy, appalled by the whole, unsavoury affair.

COLD, QUIET EMBERS

They walked together along one of several park avenues, the sound of children playing filling the air. It was as far removed from the harsh, brutal rigors of frontier life as Cole could possibly imagine. Here, in this safe haven, the war seemed a million miles away. People were full of laughter, carefree, unruffled by the news from the south. General Grant was now overall commander of the Union forces in the west and was pressing hard against the Confederate lines, having forced a breakout with his counter-attack at Wauhatchie.

But Cole was not here to talk of war. Dressed in his finest Sunday clothes, he had made the journey across country, taking a train for the first time in his life, and here he was, walking with Penelope Dryson, enjoying the warm yet fragile sunshine of that fall.

"What will you do now, Reuben?"

They stopped at a small artificial lake. Ducks were swimming across the water, other birds singing in the overhanging trees. If Cole could conjure up his idea of heaven, this would be it. And Penelope would be his guiding angel.

"I'll return to the fort," he said, leaning across the railings separating the lake from the path. "I've heard a rumour they want me to lead yet another expedition into enemy territory." He blew out his cheeks. "I hope it is the last time, Penelope, I truly do."

"I think we all wish this dreadful conflict will end soon. All of us have been so affected by it. Poor Mrs Winter, she cries herself to sleep every night, staring endlessly at the photograph of her husband."

"Is she not relieved at Sergeant Winter's exoneration?"

"Of course, but it still pains her to know that her husband was murdered by that dreadful man." She offered a grim smile and reached over to grip Cole's hand. "We can never thank you enough for all that you did, Reuben."

He returned her smile. She did not know all the details and, certainly, he did not want her to ever uncover the reality of Mathieson's shameful death. Nor what happened some days later.

The day dawned much like any other. There was a different atmosphere in the fort now. Lieutenant Owen was acting Commander and expectations of who would replace Mathieson were high. Meanwhile, preparations were being made for troops to march south and relieve Grant's Union forces entrenched around the city of Chattanooga, surrounded as they were by the Confederates under Braxton Bragg.

Orders were given. Cole would scout ahead before the column set out. Although there had been no sightings of Rebel forces nearby, nothing could be left to chance. Cole rode out alone, reading the ground for any signs. Of Rebel soldiers, he found none.

Later, he camped by a nearby brook. The weather was changing, the late afternoons much colder, and rain fell more frequently than of late. He made himself a small fire, setting a pot of coffee on the crackling wood he had gathered. After his drink, he would return to the fort.

He straightened his back, poured himself a coffee in a

dented, buckled tin cup, and sighed. "Thought you might turn up," he said quietly.

The figure emerged from the undergrowth nearby. Lathered in sweat, his clothes torn and filthy, Jessop presented a dreadful sight. Gaunt eyes sunk into his head, he was no doubt starving. He had been on the run for some weeks, having fled the fort as soon as the truth had been revealed.

"You're a dead man, Cole, and I'm gonna kill you for what you did."

Without a flicker of emotion, Cole deftly threw away his tin cup and quickly rolled over to his right. As Jessop clawed for his gun, Cole was on his knees, Navy coming up in a blur. It barked twice and Jessop, hit in the chest and throat, squawked and span, dizzy like some fairground marionette, the blood belching from his wounds. He fell onto his face with a heavy grunt and lay still.

Cole stood up, closed his eyes for a moment, a released the air from his lungs. He was no assassin. Or so he used to believe. The reality, however, spoke otherwise.

"You seem so far away, Reuben."

Blinking, Cole came back to the present and found her eyes burning into him, so much care in those azure pools of loveliness. He looked down to see her hand still grasping his.

"Penelope," he began, his voice tight, throat dry. He had rehearsed many times what he needed to say but now, with her so close, her perfume invading his nostrils, the memory of his well-practiced lines deserted him and he could only manage some garbled, incoherent utterances. "Penelope, I er, wanted to say how much ...." Exasperated, he squeezed his eyes shut. "Oh, Penelope, I wanted to say—"

"Reuben ..."

Was this the moment he longed for? Penelope coming to his rescue, aiding him to utter those words he longed to say by completing his sentence with words of her own? Words to sanctify their relationship, give the future meaning? He held his breath.

"Reuben, I have to tell you. I have met a young man. His name is Nicholas and he is a lawyer. Well, a trainee to be honest, but he is so well qualified, so diligent and professional in his undertakings. We have met several times and last week, he asked for my hand."

Around him, the world seemed to go into a whirl. He no longer heard her voice. Everything, the ducks, the birds, the gentle sunshine, faded into a murky background. He gazed at her mouth forming the words but he did not hear them. Nothing existed anymore, his love shattered and scattered to the wind.

On his return to the fort, he went about his business as usual. The forces moved down to Chattanooga and aided Grant in his breakout. Before the year was out, Confederate forces were driven back into Georgia. The tide of the war, or so it seemed, was turning at last.

He rarely thought of Penelope but sometimes, in the dead of night, her face came to him in his dreams and when he woke, his eyes were still wet from the tears he shed for a love so bitterly lost.

ABOUT THE AUTHOR

 Born on the Wirral, I live in Spain for the present, but my dream is to retire (Hah, what is that? Retire?) and live on a narrowboat along one of the many waterways around the Welsh border. I work as a teacher, a profession I've been in for almost 25 years, but writing is my first love.

To learn more about Stuart G. Yates and discover more Next Chapter authors, visit our website at www.nextchapter.pub.

Baptism of Fire
ISBN: 978-4-82415-092-9

Published by
Next Chapter
2-5-6 SANNO
SANNO BRIDGE
143-0023 Ota-Ku, Tokyo
+818035793528

15th September 2022

Ingram Content Group UK Ltd.
Milton Keynes UK
UKHW010622080323
418216UK00003B/86